Beer in the Snooker Club

WAGUIH GHALI

Waguih Ghali was born in Cairo on February 25, most likely in 1930. He attended high school in Alexandria and then studied abroad in Europe. Fearing political persecution, he fled Egypt in 1958 and lived in London, also spending time in France, Sweden, and Germany. Ghali authored several personal essays, which appeared in *The Guardian* between 1957 and 1965. He also spent time as a freelance journalist, reporting for the *Times* of London and the BBC. Following a battle with depression, Ghali committed suicide in London, at the home of his friend and editor Diana Athill, in 1969. *Beer in the Snooker Club* is his only finished novel.

INTERNATIONAL

Beer in the Snooker Club

WAGUIH GHALI

Introduction by Pankaj Mishra

VINTAGE INTERNATIONAL
Vintage Books
A Division of Random House LLC
New York

FIRST VINTAGE INTERNATIONAL EDITION, JUNE 2014

The Library of Congress has cataloged the Knopf edition as follows:
Ghali, Waguih.
Beer in the Snooker Club / Waguih Ghali.—1st American edition.
p. cm
PZ4.G425 Be   1964
64012296

Vintage Trade Paperback ISBN: 978-0-8041-7074-1
eBook ISBN: 978-0-8041-7075-8

www.vintagebooks.com

Printed in the United States of America

INTRODUCTION

"History," Stephen Dedalus says in *Ulysses*, "is a nightmare from which I am trying to awake." By the 1960s, this plangent cry was being echoed by many sensitive men and women in Asian and African countries that had only recently entered modern history as sovereign nation-states. The passionate idealism of anti-imperialist movements and the longing for justice and dignity that went into the making of many new nations had been compromised by the corruption and ineptitude of the first generation of rulers. The futile cycle of coups and countercoups, and the long game of musical chairs between military strongmen and civilian politicians, had already begun. "The politics that came," writes the disenchanted Caribbean narrator of V. S. Naipaul's *The Mimic Men* (1967), "made people aware of their pain. Later they came to see their helplessness."

Few people felt more vulnerable to this postcolonial chaos than members of the property-owning classes. These local elites had prospered during European rule, often as collaborators in a system of exploitation. Educated in Western or Western-style institutions, they had become emotionally and spiritually, as well as materially, dependent on the European metropolis, all the while growing aloof from the rest of their compatriots. After independence, they tended to see their often expensive lifestyles, no less than their power, menaced by newly assertive political movements of peasants, factory workers, and ambitious military officers. And even the most altruistic and perceptive of these native aristocrats found themselves thwarted by their remoteness from ordinary lives.

Alienation was, for them, more than a pose cheaply borrowed, along with black turtlenecks, from French existentialists. It stultified private life—a realm often defined by quietly desperate love affairs with European men and women—as well as political gestures. *The Mimic Men*, detailing a career "sunk in the taint of fantasy," was among the extraordinary spate of novels and films in Asia, Africa, and Latin America—from Driss Chraïbi's *Heirs to the Past* and Tayeb Salih's *Season of Migration to the North* to the film *Memories of Underdevelopment* by Cuban Tomás Gutiérrez Alea—that diagnosed the failure and premature exhaustion of the most

I

privileged and talented young men and women before the arduous challenges of revolution, nation building, and self-renewal. But the work of art from this era that has effortlessly assumed the authority of a classic, and has actually felt more prescient and moving since the Arab Spring, is Waguih Ghali's *Beer in the Snooker Club*.

Little is known about Ghali except that he was born into a well-off family of Coptic Christians and seems to have known intimately the radical postures and precarious bohemianism that his only novel describes with perfectly balanced harshness and solicitude. His true literary predecessor, in many ways, is Albert Cossery, who was from a Greek Orthodox bourgeois family in Cairo and who wrote in French. Cossery denounced the modern world altogether in fictions that upheld a strategic indolence as the correct response to its imperatives to think and work hard. Even the most politicized Egyptian in Cossery's 1948 novel, *Laziness in the Fertile Valley*, wonders, "Why did [men] have to struggle, always vicious and discontented, when the sole wisdom lay in a careless, passive attitude?" But Ghali belonged, like his first-person narrator, Ram, to a generation of listless youth that had been galvanized by the overthrow of Egypt's cravenly pro-British monarch Farouk in 1952 and the advent of the pan-Arab nationalist Gamal Abdel Nasser. "The only important thing," Ram says, "which happened to us was the Egyptian revolution." Yet, as his account goes on to show with unsentimental insight and acid humor, this was yet another revolution that—as Milan Kundera wrote in *Life Is Elsewhere*, another 1960s fiction about the fantasies of the romantic intellectual— had "no desire to be examined or analyzed, it only desires that the people merge with it; in this sense it is lyrical and in need of lyricism."

Revolution may have been the opiate of the brighter demimonde, but Egypt in the 1950s did possess its conditions. Its cities, especially Cairo, were overwhelmed by a massive influx of people who had fled rural subsistence economies only to face unemployment and the degradation of life in slums. The national economy was dominated by a large class of coldhearted landlords, rent seekers, and businessmen who ferreted their profits abroad rather than reinvesting them in the country. One of the wonders of *Beer in the Snooker Club* is the delicacy with which Ghali sketches a background of deprivation and anger into the confusions of a parochial elite. In what is essentially an account of drift and futility,

2

Ghali—a card-carrying Communist—is always clear about the fate of the insulted and injured people he wanted to care for.

The novel opens with Ram's aunt, a member of the "cosmopolitan" feudal class, or "parasites," as Ram's friend Font calls them, selling surplus land to the fellaheen and "pretending to the government she was giving the land to the poor." These are the Cairenes who, having migrated spiritually to the European metropolis, won't bother to learn Arabic and despise the celebrated singer Umm Kulthum. Ram himself is shown to be initially indifferent to the inequities of his society. "I was neither Red, Pink, Blue, nor Black. I had no politics in me then." His political—and sentimental—education is initiated by Edna, a Jewish member of Cairo's upper class.

Unlike Ram, Edna has successfully rebelled against her comprador origins. "I hate Egyptians of your class as much as I do my parents," she tells Ram. "It was Edna who introduced me to Egyptian people," Ram writes, adding, "it is rare, in the milieu in which I was born, to know Egyptians." He and his close friend Font hungrily start to read the books she suggests. She initiates them into the cruelties of European imperialism, and the struggles for freedom waged across the postcolonial world. "Gradually, we began to see ourselves as members of humanity in general and not just as Egyptians." One symptom of political awakening in the postcolonial world during the 1950s was anti-Americanism: Ram and Font share a "vehement phobia towards Egyptians who read the American *Time Magazine*." When Ram's America-returned cousin Mounir claims that "American Democracy is *the* thing" and pontificates about the "Red Menace," he finds himself violently challenged by Edna's intellectual protégé Ram, who has since picked up a lot of information about the plight of blacks and Native Americans in Freedom's Land.

Yet Ram can't help sense some falsity in his new role as a firebrand, and his exposure to the big world outside Egypt also breeds a different kind of appetite for life elsewhere.

> The world of ice and snow in winter and red, slanting roof-tops was beginning to call us. The world of intellectuals and underground metros and cobbled streets and a green countryside which we had never seen, beckoned to us. The world where students had rooms and

3

typists for girl-friends, and sang songs and drank beer in
large mugs, shouted to us. . . . I wanted to live. I read
and read and Edna spoke and I wanted to live. I wanted
to have affairs with countesses and to fall in love with a
barmaid and to be a gigolo and to be a political leader to
win at Monte Carlo and to be down-and-out in London
and to be an artist to be elegant and also to be in rags.

Some of these exuberant and contradictory desires are actually fulfilled
as Edna helps Ram and his friend Font travel to England—"Jesus, Font;
here we are, London and everything"—and Ram turns out to have a better
time of it than most other people from the colonies. As an exotic, he finds
himself quickly adopted by a left-leaning English family in Hampstead. His
superior class and education and fair skin help him transcend the racism
that most other colonials are subjected to. So he can pity rather than despise
the uneducated former soldier in Kilburn who calls Egyptians "wogs," and
even find it "natural" to sleep with the Englishman's fiancée. He has the
upper hand on the condescending white woman who tries to pigeonhole
him as one of the "intelligent Egyptians . . . at the Gezira Sporting Club."
Worried that he is turning into a "phoney" like his shiftless compatriots,
"the Cairo arties, who if not slumming in Europe, are driving their Jaguars in Zamalek," he imagines being "down-and-out" in the East End before
deciding against the idea. He ends up with a compromise in Battersea, living with a working-class man and his Irish stepfather.

　　Ghali recounts these adventures in Englishness with bittersweet com-
edy: the lonely London bedsits we know from the novels of Patrick Ham-
ilton and Muriel Spark are suffused here with the hopefulness and energy
of the deracinated colonial, who has been made to wait too long for life to
begin elsewhere. To a man like Ram, conditioned by his provincial background and education to revere the metropolis, London represents all
the unalloyed and thrilling glamour of metropolitan modernity; indeed,
England on the whole turns out to embody the coherent world of Europe,
where, unlike in Egypt, words hadn't drifted free from their meanings:
"where miners were communists and policemen fascists; where there was
something called the 'bourgeoisie' and someone called the 'landlady.'"

　　But the West, so seductive with its ever-renewed promise of pleasure and stability, remains a source of ambivalence to Ram. When in

4

1956 Britain tries, in a fit of neo-imperialist delirium, to militarily seize control over the Suez Canal, Ram is further radicalized.

> In spite of all the books we had read demonstrating
> the slyness and cruelty of England's foreign policy, it
> took the Suez war to make us believe it. Of course the
> Africans and the Asians had had their Suezes a long
> time before us . . . over and over again.

Ram joins the Communist Party. But he can't avoid the suspicion that he is not a political animal. He wonders to Edna if he is just someone who likes to "gamble and drink and make love." Constantly remaking himself to suit other's people expectations in London, he also comes to feel an inner incoherence—the distinctive "panic," as the dandyish narrator of Naipaul's *The Mimic Men* precisely defines it, "of ceasing to feel myself as a whole person" and of failing to "fashion order out of all these unrelated adventures and encounters, myself never the same, never even the thread on which these things were hung." Ram is appalled to discover that he is developing a split: between the external doer and the inner observer, "the one participating and the other watching and judging." More disturbing, he finds that "there is a touch of gimmick in whatever I do." Even his professions of love for Edna are haunted by an oppressive sense of déjà vu: "a scene probably already encountered in a film or a play." He can't get rid of the feeling that "I have lost my natural self. I have become a character in a book."

This loss of spontaneous feeling would seem less consequential—a personal flaw at most—if it didn't also preclude original thinking in a postcolonial society still ruled by nostrums imported from abroad. "The revolt of the Third World," Octavio Paz once warned, "has degenerated into different varieties of frenzied Caesarism or languishes beneath the stranglehold of bureaucracies that are both cynical and fuzzy-minded." New nation-states had become prone to despotism largely because the revolt against the West had "not discovered its proper form"—ideas and institutions suited to indigenous realities. Its political and intellectual leaders suffered from a " 'split personality,' or in moral terms, 'inauthenticity.' " They invoked "modern ideas"—revolution, freedom, democracy, socialism, industrialization, mass literacy—but "these ideas in many cases have been mere superficial borrowings: they have not been instruments of liberation but masks. Like all masks, their function is to

5

shield us from the gaze of others, and, by a circular process that has often been described, to shield us from our own gaze."

Ram is aware that he must find a life for himself; but, sunk in the taint of colonial fantasy, and obscured by the masks of modern ideas, this basic task of self-definition is harder for him than for the Egyptian people he seeks to represent. Yes, he has joined the Communist Party, but, as he admits, only because he can't do anything else with his knowledge of suffering and injustice. Returning to Egypt, where the parasites, it turns out, "hadn't been dealt a heavy blow by the revolution," the fellaheen remain exposed to exploitation, communists have been imprisoned, and Edna has become victim to the bigotry that would soon rid Cairo of most of its Jewish, Greek, and Armenian population, Ram and Font drift into another kind of playacting: this time, as superfluous intellectuals.

Font finds a job "brushing the snooker tables with the Literary Supplement." Ram tries his hand at human-rights activism. But no newspaper wants to publish his evidence of torture in Egyptian prisons. Furthermore, Ram has "the terrible feeling that some of the pictures wouldn't be so gory if we didn't pay for them." His most sincere act seems to be drinking homemade "Bass"—a cocktail of the Egyptian beer Stella, vodka, and whisky—in a snooker club, or trying to *épater le bourgeois* by pushing Mounir, the slick America-phile, into the swimming pool of the Gezira Sporting Club. Even the anti-Americanism is now a brittle affair, undermined by the irrecoverable colonial's self-pity: "We're so English it is nauseating. We have no culture of our own." "The mental sophistication of Europe," Ram concludes, "has killed something good and natural in us, killed it for good . . . for ever." He even longs for the "blissful ignorance" of the time before he met Edna. "Wasn't it nice to go to the Catholic church with my mother before I ever heard of Salazar or of the blessed troops to Ethiopia?"

"I never realized I had made you so lonely," says Edna, and this impossible love between a radical Jewish woman and a Coptic intellectual manqué, both abandoned by history as well as by their gods, is the aching heart of this novel. However psychologically damaged and denuded of genuine emotion, Ram achieves a tragic intensity in his feelings for Edna: "I saw her bullied by nationalities and races and political events and revolutions and dictatorships and particularly by her own vague idealism. I held her tenderly in my arms and also saw my own shallowness and unworthiness in contrast to her deepness and sincerity."

But Ram is also aware that he is "never really natural" with Edna, and she knows he won't be happy with her. As the novel ends, Ram moves to marry a rich heiress he has flirted with previously. He confesses he wants to live in a "beautiful house with lots of books bound in leather." "You know me better," he finds himself saying, "than to think I'd sacrifice my comfort or life or anything." This may seem an excessively cynical and dramatic conversion to bourgeois ease. But Ram is acting out what to us in the early twenty-first century is a demoralizingly well-known script. How often have we met the Western-educated scion of a wealthy or powerful family in the postcolonial world, who speaks with beguiling passion of democracy and human rights and women's education, and then at the first sign of any threat to his privileged lifestyle retreats quickly into the prejudices of his class?

Recent years have also made many of us familiar with the "polished products of the English 'Left'" or their contemporary version, the adepts of Western social media and digital radicalism, who are "lonely and without lustre in the budding revolution of the Arab world." Ghali and his generation of westernized intellectuals were the first to confront the brute reality that the budding revolution they passionately supported could not bloom. Ghali, pitilessly anatomizing the dilettante upper-class activist, seems to have also understood the reasons behind his political impotence and despair: Egypt, like many countries damaged by colonialism, was condemned to decades of economic subordination and geopolitical compromise abroad, as well as a futile circulation of ruthlessly self-serving elites at home. Not surprisingly, Ram chooses, like the hero of Albert Cossery's last novel, *The Colors of Infamy* (1999), "merely to survive in a society ruled by crooks, without waiting for the revolution, which was hypothetical and continually being put off until tomorrow."

"By hiding us from others," Ocatvio Paz had warned the Third World's intellectuals, "the mask also hides us from ourselves." But such self-deception wasn't Ghali's burden. In his ability to see through private and political impostures, and to violate the genteel protocol of much fiction produced by the postcolonial bourgeoisie, he has no peers, not even Naipaul and the great Cossery, who had intuited early the curse of underdevelopment in Egypt. Rather, Ghali's cruel fate was to pay in his own life the devastating psychic costs of a near-permanent political impasse.

7

Threatened with arrest for being a communist, Ghali had been forced to leave Egypt in 1958. His passport expired in London. Unable to return to Egypt or stay in England, he went into exile in Germany, where he wrote *Beer in the Snooker Club* while working in a factory. He began a second novel, ostensibly about the misery of being a "guest worker" in Europe's greatest postwar "miracle" economy, on his return to London in 1966; but he never finished it. Whatever happened in Egypt—and by the late 1960s, the spell of Nasser over the Egyptian masses had broken—or Europe, history was going to remain a nightmare for him; his attempt to awaken from it would never succeed. All he could hope to do was douse the ferociously warring impulses inside him.

"What are you, Ram?" Edna asks at one point in *Beer in the Snooker Club*. He replies, "I am insincere, but honest." The confession—substituting authenticity for sincerity—is the key to the novel, its author's tormented life, and the manner of his death. On the night of Boxing Day 1969, Ghali wrote in his diary:

> I am going to kill myself tonight. . . . The time has come. I am, of course, drunk. But then sober it would have been very very very difficult. (I acknowledge the drunken writing myself.) But what else could I do, sweethearts? loved ones? Nothing, really. Nothing.

A scrupulous observer to the last of his innermost turmoil, Ghali swallowed twenty-six sleeping pills, then wrote: "And the most dramatic moment of my life—the only authentic one—is a terrible let-down." But Ghali knew, in this terrible instant of perfect lucidity, that he finally had his only chance of moving out of the stalled dialectic of insincerity and honesty, and into a much-longed-for peace. "I have already swallowed my death," he added. "I could vomit it out if I wanted to." But:

> Honestly and sincerely, I really don't want to. It is a pleasure. I am doing this not in a sad, unhappy way; but on the contrary, happily and even (a state of being and a word I have always loved) SERENELY . . . serenely.

Pankaj Mishra
2014

8

PART I

Rather, we aim at being personalities of a general . . . a fictitious type.

DOSTOIEVSKY

I watched my aunt signing papers. Three hundred or more in a neat pack in front of her, her secretary standing behind her taking one sheet at a time as it was signed, and forming another neat pack of signed sheets. She gave me a look in between signatures. I must have disturbed her.

She was giving away three acres of land at each signature, and an acre of land in our country is a lot of money. Her name would be in the papers next day for kindness and generosity to the poor. And it should be, too, when she was giving all that away.

I had a cigarette but no matches. I put it in my mouth and tried to attract the secretary's attention. I waited, my courage increasing. I decided to wait until she had signed another ten thousand pounds' worth before asking for a match. One . . . two . . . three . . . four . . . about five thousand pounds; five . . . six . . . seven . . . 'May I have a light, Hassan Effendi?'

She didn't hear me, neither did Hassan Effendi. He didn't even look round. There on the table was a lighter, a big silver Ronson – Aladdin's lamp. I edged towards the table. One step and I was there. In another instant it was in my hands. Tick tick. It didn't work. She murmured something to Hassan Effendi. He put his hand in his pocket and gave me a new box of matches.

I looked at the clock. Twenty past nine. In another ten minutes I would have been there for an hour and a half. I smoked. The pack of signed sheets increased, the other pack decreased. About fifty more, I estimated. She must be tired, poor woman, signing a thousand papers a day and this her third day. I felt for her; a woman with ten thousand acres to look after – but happily the régime allowed her only two hundred now. I remembered how, once, in Europe, she gave me a five-pound note.

Then Marie came in. She is a good soul, Marie, a good friend of the family: helps here and there during receptions, always present during illness, always remembering birthdays. She doesn't know when my birthday falls, or that of my mother, but then we have never told her.

'Hello, Ram,' she said, sitting beside me, 'what are you doing here?'

'Come to borrow money.'

She didn't say anything. She has money of her own, and when you are in my situation, it's best to speak out, specially to those who have money. It makes them feel closer knit to each other and all that, and then, of course, you can never tell.

I felt sorry for Marie. She wants to speak very much; to tell me she hopes I get the money and to ask me why I want it – particularly to ask me that. But her position is delicate. She bought a new Cadillac two days ago and it would be vulgar to mention money right now. I looked at her and smiled.

'How is your mother?' she asked.

'She's very sick,' I lied.

This was bound to keep her quiet for another ten minutes at least. I was more interested in my paper-signing aunt. The way I looked at it, if she was giving away a million pounds' worth of land to no matter whom, she'd give me a thousand pounds. Particularly if I hinted that I'd leave the country if I had that much.

I looked at my aunt, then at the clock, and finally at Marie.

'Hello, Marie,' I said. 'You're-looking-very-well-how-is-your-new-car?'

She looked at me with tenderness. 'You're so thoughtful, my sweet. It's not bad. The other one was costing me so much in petrol, I simply couldn't afford it. Had to buy a new one.'

A small commotion at the desk. The signing had ended for the day.

'*Tiens*,' said my aunt. 'I didn't notice you come in, Marie. Ouf! I am fed up with this signing. You must be tired too, Hassan Effendi. But it is the least we can do for these poor devils, the fellaheen.' That was good. I tried to look as much fellah as possible.

'Wait a minute, Marie, I'm coming back in a moment.' My aunt went out, followed by Hassan Effendi carrying a thousand sheets worth a million pounds; or perhaps not quite a million pounds, because she was selling cheap and pretending to the government she was giving the land to the poor.

'Hello, hello, Marie', I said again.

'Tell me,' she asked, 'are you in business now?'

I told her I had discovered a brand-new way of exploiting the fellah. All I needed was capital.

'You mustn't joke about such things, dearie,' she said.

My aunt came back and said the price of bread had increased by half a piastre. This affected them both very much because they buy bread every day. I tried to be as helpful as possible and told them of a baker I know who sells bread wholesale and by weight. Then I told them how to heat stale bread in the oven, but got muddled trying to deduct the price of the gas used to heat the oven from the money they would save by heating the stale bread. I was going to

13

tell them how to jump off the tram at Abbasieh and not pay for a ticket, but thought better of it. I went outside the room for a moment and stuck my ear to the keyhole.

'Be careful,' Marie was telling my aunt, 'he's come to borrow money.'

'I know, my dear. That's why I telephoned you. He won't dare ask me in your presence.'

I left and went to Groppi's. I drank whisky and ate peanuts, watching the sophisticated crowd and feeling happy that my aunt had refused to give me the money. I had asked simply because my conscience was nagging. It was something I vaguely had to do but had kept putting off. Soon Omar and Jameel came in, then Yehia, Fawzi and Ismail. Groppi's is perhaps one of the most beautiful places to drink whisky in. The bar is under a large tree in the garden and there is a handsome black barman who speaks seven languages. We drank a bottle of whisky between us and I watched them fight to pay for it. Yehia paid, then we all left together. They each possess a car.

I am always a bit bored in the mornings because they are all either at the university or working. Sometimes I go and play snooker with Jameel at the billiards' club. You can find him there anytime – in fact he owns it. I would go there more often if it weren't for Font. Whenever I reproach myself for drinking too much, I tell myself it's Font who is driving me to drink. 'Font,' I told him once, 'just tell me what you want me to do?'

'Run away, you scum,' he answered. So I went to Groppi's and drank more whisky. There you are, although, of course, I still read *The New Statesman* and *The Guardian* and

14

mine is perhaps the only copy of *Tribune* which comes to Egypt.

'Font,' I said another time, when I was nicely oiled and in a good mood, 'Font,' I said, 'you're about the only angry young man in Egypt.' And I laughed. It struck me as very funny.

'Go,' he replied. 'Go and sponge some more on these parasites.'

It was I who made Font work in the snooker club. Jameel thought I was joking when I told him it was the only thing would keep Font off the streets. In fact I had to show him Font with his barrow in Sharia-el-Sakia. Jameel was shocked to see one of his old school-friends on the street. It was all I could do to stop him from offering Font enough money to live on for the rest of his life. Font would have spat on him and probably hit me.

There he was then. Selling cucumbers. Cucumbers of all things. Of course I understood. He was Jimmy Porter. We had seen the play together in London and there he was, a degree in his pocket and selling cucumbers. There were other barrows too; lettuce, onions, sunflower seeds, beans. We stopped the car in front of Font and looked at him.

'Get going,' he said.

I said I wanted to buy cucumbers but that I didn't trust his weights.

'Scram,' he shouted. 'I'll break your rotten face if you don't scram.' (This is typical Font. He'll be sarcastic to the other boys but when it's me, he's infuriated.) Jameel told him he needed someone to look after the snooker place for him.

'He's too much of a snob,' I said. 'He wouldn't like to

be seen working where his old school-friends might come in.'

'Do you think I give a damn about you idiots,' Font screamed. Jameel is a quiet fellow and told him he really needed someone. Font might have accepted if I had not been there, so he looked at me with his 'you dirty traitor' expression instead.

'Font,' I asked in English, 'what do the other barrow boys think of Virginia Woolf?'

He fell into the trap and answered in English.

'You making fun of them? They never had a chance to go to school, you scum. Has that parasite beside you ever read a book in his life? With all his money he's nothing but a fat, ignorant pig.'

Jameel is so docile he doesn't mind being called a fat, ignorant pig at all. However, by then the other barrow boys were approaching. Font, dressed in Arab clothes, looking after a barrow and speaking in English, awoke their curiosity. 'What's that? What's that?' they asked.

'He's a spy,' I told them and they immediately became threatening. 'We'll deal with that son of a dog,' they shouted. Font became incoherent with rage. We pulled him into the car and drove away quickly.

I had to leave the car soon afterwards to escape Font's wrath, but a week later he was brushing the snooker tables with the *Literary Supplement*.

I went from Groppi's to the snooker club. It is a large place with thick carpets in between the tables, a cosy bar and deep leather armchairs. It impresses with its subdued luxury and, one feels, bad manners would be sacrilege there.

Jameel's father having accepted defeat in educating his son, gave way to the boy's passion for snooker and built this place for him; which turned out to be excellent business. He is a strange man, Jameel's father. Believe it or not, he's a sincere socialist, a genuine one. Not a rich 'Liberal' nor a wealthy *The Nation* reader; no, he is active in his ideas and was once imprisoned by Farouk's gang. He often comes for a game: a tall, lean, elegant man who had a French education and who writes to *L'Express* of France. I like Dr Hamza; as a matter of fact I'd like to be like him: well-dressed and soberly aristocratic and having been imprisoned for socialist views. I would not like to *go* to prison, but I'd like to have been. Of course Font isn't going to be patronized and Dr Hamza isn't going to be patronizing; so there is a layer of sympathy separating them.

As I said, I went to the snooker club. I went behind the bar and watched Font run the vacuum cleaner over the carpets. There is a perpetual look of amazement on Font's face which makes one want to answer an unasked question. The way he works the vacuum cleaner over the carpets with his eyebrows uplifted and his eyes wide, probing into the difficult turns and corners between tables, gives the impression that if he could only get the machine into *that* particular corner, he'd find the answer to whatever was puzzling him.

'Draught Bass, Font?'

'Yes, all right.'

I opened two bottles of Egyptian Stella beer and poured them into a large tumbler, then beat the liquid until all the gas had escaped. I then added a drop of vodka and some whisky. It was the nearest we could get to Draught Bass.

There is a street off the Edgware Road in London, where a gang of Teddy boys, Irish labourers and other odds and ends used to play dice on the pavement. We Egyptians are gamblers. Wherever Egyptians are gathered, you can be sure that sooner or later they'll start gambling. It's not that we want to win money or anything, we just like to gamble. We're lazy and we like to laugh. It's only when gambling that we are wide awake and working hard. Font and I won a lot of money on that pavement once, and went to a silversmith in Edgware Road and bought the two silver beer mugs we now keep behind the snooker club bar. We had our names engraved on them and vowed to drink nothing but Draught Bass from them. I now poured my concoction into the mugs and waited for Font to switch the sweeper off.

'It's not bad,' Font said. 'How much did you make?'

'About two pints each.'

'I'm going to be nicely boozed all day.'

'I'll spend the day here, too,' I said.

If Font hadn't been so lonely, he would never have spoken to me. But he is lonely and he wants to discuss something with me; I knew that, or I would have known better than to come and chat with him.

'The real trouble with us,' he said (when Font says 'us' for him and me, it means he's exceptionally kindly disposed towards me), 'is that we're so English it is nauseating. We have no culture of our own.'

'Speak for yourself,' I said. 'I can crack jokes with the best of Egyptians.'

'Perhaps you're right,' he said. 'Perhaps our culture is nothing but jokes.'

'No, Font, it isn't. It's just that we have never learnt Arabic properly.' That is the way I have to speak to Font. I have to contradict him, at least in the early part of any day we are to spend together, and I have to speak slowly or he'll accuse me of trying to be eloquent instead of carrying on an ordinary conversation.

'Then what do you mean by saying that cracking jokes is culture?'

'What I mean is,' I replied, 'that jokes to Egyptians are as much culture as calypso is to West Indians, or as spirituals and jazz to American Negroes. In fact,' I continued, saying whatever came to my mouth, for that is the way to coax Font into trusting my sincerity, 'it is no less culture than playing the organ is culture.'

I filled our beer mugs again and started preparing some more Bass. Font pondered over what I had just said. I sometimes say such things and then a moment later they sound less silly than they do when I utter them.

It was past eleven, and the first two customers came in; Arevian and Doromian, two rich Armenians who own the shoe-store downstairs. Two fat and greasy individuals with a sense of humour.

'Good day, good day, professors,' they said to Font and me (Font's degree is a source of great amusement to them). 'We have come to play marbles for your amusement, Herr Doctor Professor Font. It is the ambition of our humble life to divert your knowledgeable eyes with our childish efforts, thus allowing your brain to dwell upon lofty matters.' They bowed down to Font and made as though to kiss his hands – an ancient custom in government circles.

'Look at them,' Font said, 'they pay that miserable man

19

downstairs six pounds a month to work twelve hours a day for them, and then they come here and gamble for thousands as though for peanuts.'

'Forgive us, forgive us, Herr Doctor,' Doromian sang. 'If our Hassan had so much as a minor degree from Heidelberg or the Sorbonne, we would give him . . . eight pounds.'

When I said they owned the shoe-store downstairs, I wasn't quite exact. One of them owns it and the other has lost it. They play for fantastic amounts of money, and when money has been exhausted, they play for their share of the shop. They never lend money to one another. I remember Doromian losing everything including his car, and Arevian refusing to lend him the price of the tram home.

Font started laying out the snooker balls for them. I finished two pints of this Bass which makes me comfortable and allows my Oriental brain to wonder over non-Oriental things such as Font, and other Fonts I've known, and even the Font that I am myself at times. Fonts who are not Keir Hardies but Jimmy Porters in the Egyptian Victorian age; Fonts who are not revolutionaries or leaders in the class struggle, but polished products of the English 'Left', lonely and without lustre in the budding revolution of the Arab world.

These thoughts on the one hand and on the other the pleasure in sitting in Groppi's and drinking whisky without having to pay for it, or of coming to the snooker club and sitting within reach of the bottles. Thinking of this, I reached out and swung the Martell bottle to my lips. Life was good.

Font came back, the Bass having lowered his eyebrows somewhat. He asked me if I had seen Didi Nackla since London.

'No,' I said.

'I saw Edna and Levy yesterday,' he began. 'They are coming to my place tonight. You come too.'

Levy and Edna . . . and Font. I wish they would all leave the country and leave me alone. Levy and Edna, especially Edna. I turned round and was going to have another swig at the bottle when he stopped me.

'Don't be such a bloody coward,' he said.

I sighed and drank my beer instead.

'I haven't seen Edna for such a long time.'

'You can see her tonight.'

'I don't want to.'

'Well, don't come then.'

'You know very well I'm coming,' I said.

He smiled.

'I hope we're all chucked in jail,' I said. 'Somewhere on the Red Sea. The four of us. Then you'll really have something to be angry about. I can just see your eyebrows raised to the back of your head in amazement.'

'What do you mean?' he asked. 'Why should we be chucked in jail?' His eyebrows started rising again. 'Are you involved in something . . .?'

'No,' I said.

'Ram . . .'

'I've told you a hundred times, no.'

I longed to see Edna again. Her long, auburn hair and large, brown eyes. We'd both sit on the floor, myself behind her, Arab fashion, combing her hair. One long stroke after another, then a parting and two long plaits with a bit of string tied to the end of each plait.

'Let's talk about something else,' I said. 'Let's have another Bass.' I shared the remaining Bass and watched his eyebrows go up before he spoke.

'Did you read what he did?'

'Who?'

'Gaitskell.'

'Gaitskell. Gaitskell! For God's sake, Font, do you think I'm going to worry about . . .' and then I saw the lonely look on Font's face. 'Yes, I know,' I said. 'What do you expect? So many years being a politician, you end up by being a politician.'

'It's not true,' he shouted, 'look at Konni Zilliacus, look at Fenner Brockway . . .'

'Stop shouting, Font.' Three men had just come in and were looking at us. 'Go,' I said. 'Go and fix them some balls.' He took some keys from behind the bar and went unsteadily towards them. I was getting drunk. I took another mouthful of Martell and lit a cigarette.

The ludicrous position of an Egyptian sitting in Cairo and being furious because of Gaitskell's stand on the manufacture of nuclear weapons in England doesn't strike Font. Admittedly he began by being furious about Egyptian internal politics as well, but that too was ludicrous, like a Lucky Jim would have been in England during Dickens's time. It was like trying to ice a cake while it was still in the oven. Font knows how to trim the cake, and frost it, and garnish it with the latest decorations, but he doesn't know how to bake the cake. So he has to wait for Nasser to bake it for him before he can add his own refinements – and he's not too sure that he will be allowed to do that, even later on. In the meantime he sits and judges all the cooked cakes and hopes that the Egyptian, or Arab, cake, is going to come out the correct *shape*.

I have this silly habit of suddenly laughing. I actually saw the cake in my imagination, and it was not as flat and smooth on the surface as I would have wished. I saw myself nibbling at it here and there. Of course by then I was drunk and this cake business was very funny, especially the nibbling. I laughed out loud.

'Hoy, professor,' shouted Arevian, 'are we amusing your loftiness?'

'Did you ever meet Gaitskell, Arevian?' I shouted back.

'Of course,' he answered, pocketing a ball, 'Gaitskellian the great Armenian.'

'And Dr Summerskillian and Lord Stansgatian and Kingsley Martinian; do you know them all?'

'Played snooker with them all,' he said.

I left the snooker club without looking at Font. I was drunk again and wanted to find something to do before I became depressed. I took a bus home.

We have a pretty flat overlooking the Nile at Zamalek. It is strange, but I have never asked my mother how much money she has. We have this pretty flat and we seem to be eating as well as ever.

'Tu as essayé de t' employer?' she asked.

'Penses-tu.' Of course she spoke French, and *t'employer* she said, not *chercher du travail.*

I am not working. I haven't been working since I came back from Europe. Don't think I have any money, though; I haven't, nor do I have a father to support me. In fact to possess a father in Egypt is an uncommon luxury. Our mothers are legally married and all that, but their husbands die young, the average age being thirty-five or thereabouts. My mother took me to live with her parents when I was four. By the time I was seven, there were three widowed aunts and eight orphans living with Grandfather and Grandmother (people like my grandparents raise the average age somewhat). The fact that my aunts were very rich but not my mother, never occurred to me. I drifted on that rich tide. I was as well dressed as the other orphans and went to the same school. Each orphan was expensively equipped and was sent to England, France or Switzerland as soon as he matriculated. When my turn came, however, I was rather coldly eyed by one aunt after another and I had to realize that the tide had dissipated and that I didn't possess locomotion of my own. So now I am drifting on the tide of my school friends. Why, they themselves wouldn't have it otherwise. Honestly, this word 'sponging' is as disgusting to me as it is to Font. If you want the truth, when I came back I thought that Nasser had finally blown a magic air and that all tides had vanished. I would have worked then if I could have got as much money as my friends. As it is, if I work I would have to leave my rich friends, and I *like* my friends.

I rang up Assam the Turk. His sister answered.

'Hello, Zouzou; is Assam there?'

'No,' she answered, 'I suppose you're looking for a game?'

'Don't be silly, Zouzou; you know I don't gamble any

more.' My mother heard the word 'gamble' and came running to hear the conversation.

'Well, he isn't here,' Zouzou said, 'but I'll tell you where he is if you promise me something.'

'I promise.'

'Tell him to take me to the ball at the Semiramis next Saturday.'

'Why don't you go with your friends?'

'You know what we Turks are like,' she said, 'I'm lucky they let me go at all.'

'I thought you Turks were modernized forty years ago. You're all American now and members of NATO.'

'What's that?' she asked.

'Nothing, I was only joking. Yes, I promise to tell him. Where is he?'

'He's at Nackla Pasha's.'

'Thanks, Zouzou.'

'Listen.'

'Yes?'

'It's baccarat they're playing, not poker.'

'How do you know?'

'He borrowed a hundred pounds from me, that's how I know.'

'Thanks, Zouzou; good-bye.' My mother waited for me to explain.

'So it's baccarat they play now,' she said. 'Well, well. Assam will take all their money. He has wonderful luck, that boy.'

'I have better luck,' I said.

'Yes, your luck's not too bad either. Of course there is no question of you gambling any more.'

'No,' I said.

'Where are they playing?'

'At the Nacklas.'

'*Pas possible!* . . . has it come to that? Le Nackla playing with boys of your age?'

'No,' I said, 'unfortunately it hasn't come to that yet, although it is time it did. No,' I said, the alcohol making me angry, 'this is only a little aperitif for le Nackla. Just a few hundred pounds to amuse the young with. Later on in the evening the real thing will come.'

'But what are you getting angry at?' my mother asked.

'You're sweet, Mummy, but you don't understand. Le Nackla has no right to have all that money.'

'But it is like that all over the world,' she said.

'No, Mummy, it isn't. It isn't like that in . . .' I was going to say Russia or China, but if I did, my mother would be terrified to think I was a communist. Not that communism alarms her – she doesn't know what it is – but she has heard that communists are imprisoned and tortured, and my aunt tells her they are murderers . . . with a hint that I am one of them.

'Not like that where?' she asked suspiciously.

'In Luxemburg,' I said. 'Come, Mummy, let's have a cold beer and eat. I'm very hungry.'

She asked me whether I had seen Font lately; '*ce brave garçon*', what had happened to him? wasn't it tragic, going mad like that all of a sudden? But really I must tell her what happened during those four years in London. Didn't I feel responsible? After all it was I who talked him into going with me. How we ever managed to do it without a penny between us is a mystery of course. Is it true what people said? That we worked as ordinary labourers there? Of course she had never believed it . . . her own son . . .

London came back to me, those four years with Font, and I really became miserable. I drank more beer; it was ice-cold and all of a sudden I felt so fed up with everything that I picked up my beer glass and smashed it and we went over the same old scene again: go back to London if you're not happy here, I'll find the money somehow . . . perhaps your aunt . . . what is it really? Did I love a girl there? and so on and so on. It wasn't the first time.

'Go,' she said, 'go to the Nacklas and gamble.'

I would have gone; but it meant seeing Didi Nackla. The last time I had seen her was in London and since my return I have evaded seeing her. I don't know why. She probably thinks I am still abroad.

'No,' I said, and apologized for smashing the glass.

I slept till five in the afternoon.

'Try and find something to do, dear,' my mother said. 'Public relations or something like that would just suit you.'

'Yes, Mummy.'

'After all,' she said, 'we don't even have a car; aren't you ashamed to see your own mother ride the trams?'

'Yes,' I said..

I kissed her then went to Groppi's. I walked because I didn't have the bus fare. Ragab the barman poured me a whisky as soon as he saw me.

'They were all here and said they'll be back at seven,' he told me. It was six, which meant I had to wait until some-one came to pay for my whisky . . . or many whiskies, if I were to wait for an hour. There were three or four people sitting at the bar. One was a young man of my age reading a magazine. It had a glossy coloured cover which meant it was American. From the way he was reading it, absorbed and keen, I knew what it was. The one thing Font and I still have in common is our vehement phobia towards Egyptians who read the American *Time Magazine*. We call them Dullesian, which we consider the ultimate insult. They are well-dressed, the *Time* readers, and are called 'educated' by the American colony and journalists. They make me sick.

I had another whisky and began to feel well again. I was worrying about seeing Edna later on. No, not worrying, but afraid. No, not really afraid, but ashamed. Yes, ashamed is right. Ragab's shift behind the bar was ending and he collected the money from his customers. He didn't look at me, but whispered to his colleague and I saw him place my bill in a glass behind the bar. So even Ragab was in the secret conspiracy to keep my worklessness respectable; or had my friends told him to keep my bills for them? I didn't know. I didn't care either.

I caught the new barman's eye. He immediately started pouring me another whisky. I took my glass and sat on a cushioned bamboo armchair, having idiotically put out my tongue at the *Time* reader who looked at me as I moved. Groppi's was by then packed with people, all well-dressed and magnanimous with their orders. I was annoyed that all these people hadn't been dealt a heavy blow by the revolution. Why did they continue speaking in French? They all moan of not having enough money now, but they still live in the style they were accustomed to.

Jameel and Yehia came. The only striking thing about Jameel is his hair; not the hair itself, but the way he wears it. He has a parting in the middle. This helps keep his face characterless and benign.

'We were at the club,' he said. 'Two beautiful ones arrived today. German and Norwegian.'

The club is the Gezira Sporting Club, and the 'ones' are nurses or governesses or whatever you want to call them. 'Top' Egyptians still have foreign governesses for their children, although nowadays the governesses are pretty girls in their twenties who come for a year or so and have an expensive time with – although I hate the word – the 'bloods'.

'Yehia,' I asked, 'do you know that chap sitting behind me at the bar reading a magazine?'

'That's Coco, don't you know him? He works at General Motors. His father is . . .'

'Never mind,' I said.

'What are you having?' Jameel asked.

'I've already had three whiskies.'

'That's all right.' He waved his hand nonchalantly and went to the bar.

'What are you doing tonight?' Yehia asked.

'I'm going to Font's.'

'So you won't be using the . . .'

'No,' I answered. Six of us share a flat in town with nothing but beds in it, and dirty sheets. I say 'share' although I have never paid anything towards it.

'Are you using your car tonight, Yehia?'

'No, we're taking Jameel's. You can have mine.' He gave me the keys as Jameel came with three whiskies.

Someday, I thought, one of them is going to refuse to pay for my drinks or to lend me his car or something like that, and I shall never see them again.

'What's the matter, Jameel?' He was nervous and started to speak to me twice but changed his mind.

'Nothing important, really.'

'Go on.'

'Font was drunk today.' There was silence for a while.

'Why don't you throw him out?'

'I can't do that, Ram. We're all fond of him.'

'Anyway, what's it got to do with me?'

Yehia started smiling. 'Do you know what he did? He hit Arevian with a snooker stick. I never laughed so much. They kept running round the tables and every now and then *whizz*, the stick came down on Arevian's back. Arevian was screaming at the top of his voice and kept shouting brand-new Armenian words. Doromian was encouraging Font and nearly died laughing.'

Jameel started laughing too, and now they were both roaring. They stopped laughing after a while and told me what had happened. Doromian had spent ten minutes thinking of a way to pocket a ball from an impossible position. Of course Arevian was full of sarcasm; 'you couldn't pocket that ball in a well', and 'even if you picked it up with your fat hands it would be difficult'. Everyone, including Font, was watching. Finally Arevian said he'd burn a ten-pound note if the ball was pocketed from that position. By an amazing fluke the ball trickled into a pocket, whereupon Arevian took a ten-pound note from his wallet, lit a match and started burning the note. This enraged Font who took a snooker stick and started beating him.

I laughed. 'Frankly, Jameel,' I said, 'if you want to complain about Font don't come to me.'

'No, really, I'm not complaining. If he could only . . . I mean he should be a little . . .' and he tapered off into nothing.

Font has two rooms behind the Citadel in old Cairo. His neighbours are barrow–keepers, servants, and sometimes beggars. It is the prettiest and most colourful part of Cairo and anywhere else the arties would have flocked to it, but not in Cairo. The Cairo arties, if not slumming in Europe, are driving their Jaguars in Zamalek. I would like to live in that part of Cairo; I genuinely would prefer to live there. But with me it would be gimmicky. There is a touch of gimmick in whatever I do.

I was feeling relaxed and cheerful as I drove to Font's. Four whiskies drunk in the space of an hour and a half have that effect on me. What am I worrying about? Edna and all that? How silly. I'm free to do whatever I want. *Au fond* I don't see why I put up with Font's sneers and jeers. I won't get angry of course, but I'll . . . well, tell him to stop it. As for putting out my tongue at *Time* readers and such, it's too childish. It's time I pulled myself together. I'll even talk to my cousin Mounir and he'll manage to squeeze me into Shell or Canadian Insurance or something like that. Yes, I'll give up that other business. I'll get caught one day and have my nails pulled out. Yes, I've had a long holiday and sowed my wild Quaker oats and Fabian rubbish and now it's time for maturity, etc, etc. No, there is no reason to go to Font's and meet them with any feeling of guilt. Guilt? Guilt for what? For not letting Edna rule my life?

I drove away from Font's address, back to it and away again. It is nice to drive with a little whisky in me. When I haven't been smoking for an hour or so, and I have been drinking and then smoke, the cigarette suddenly depresses me. (It's the same with hangovers. No matter how much I've been drinking the night before, I wake up in the best of spirits, but as soon as I smoke, I am all depressed.) I stopped the car and lit a cigarette.

. . . For not letting Edna rule my life? What life, for heaven's sake? Call this a life? Call this a man?

I took more time than necessary to park the car in front of the house where Font lives; half of it on the pavement, otherwise there would be no room for other cars to pass. I put the radio on to listen to the news and finish my cigarette before going upstairs. A little boy watched me lock the car.

'I'll look after it for you,' he said.

'It's all right,' I said. 'Don't bother.'

'I'll polish it too,' he promised.

'All right,' I said and started going upstairs. Then I returned to the car and told him he could sit inside if he wished. I unlocked it and showed him how to work the radio. He was thrilled; his bare feet contracted with shyness.

'I'll clean every bit of it,' he said.

'Thank you very much,' I said and went upstairs.

Edna was sitting looking out of the window, with a cup of coffee in her hand. She was well dressed in a black suit, her elegant legs crossed. She didn't turn when I came in. I shook hands with Levy who was helping Font wash up some dishes in a corner. Levy is tall. He thrusts his head forward, his chin horizontal, giving the impression that this is the only position to keep his spectacles from falling off. In contrast to Font, Levy's eyebrows are pushed as far down as possible. I watched him dry the dishes, his movements awkward and absent-minded. There was something pathetic in the scene: Font handing Levy the dishes and Levy taking them, each with his own type of puzzled expression, a strange virus having struck them both and the symptoms of the disease so apparent. A silent *why?* on their faces. If you asked them why *what?* they would not be able to answer precisely.

I took a chair and sat half-facing Edna.

'It was, therefore,' Levy was telling Font, 'both criminal and stupid.' Levy is a product of one of the French Lycées in Egypt. This becomes obvious when he is with either Font or myself. Compared to our English education sloppiness and vagueness, his clarity in thought and speech is conspicuous.

'But do you think England and France would have attacked us if Israel had refused to participate?' Font asked.

'Yes, and Israel would have attacked without the *active* participation of England and France. If Israel had added her voice to that of the Arabs in protesting against the troop concentration in Cyprus, and had told the Arab people: whatever our differences, we shall not be an instrument of imperial designs on you, an inestimable amount of good would have been done.'

'Yes, yes; but all your "ifs" are nonsense. You know very well that all Israelis would like to see us dominated by Europe or America. Your "if" hasn't got a leg to stand on.'

Levy was hurt at this. He is always being hurt anyhow.

33

'It is a fact, Font,' he said, 'that a very large number of people in Israel objected to the Suez aggression. There is a large number of sincere socialists in Israel.'

'Sincere socialists! I know your sincere socialists. Maurice Edelman – there is your sincere socialist.'

I smiled. Maurice Edelman is a very handy name for us when discussing socialism with Jews.

'Don't take him as an example,' Levy said, 'there are people like Victor Gollancz.'

Font has a weak spot for Victor Gollancz. 'Victor Gollancz is not an Israeli,' he muttered.

'And neither is Edelman.'

Those two can go on like that for hours. With English personalities as a nucleus, they circle round and round, unaware that it is the Middle East they are discussing and not the United Kingdom.

I stopped listening to them and turned to Edna. I wondered whether Font and Levy were sexless. I wondered whether one has to be sexless to be completely sincere. I knew they had never considered Edna as a woman to be physically possessed. Doromian the Armenian once said that most men have their brains in their instruments and I wondered why Freud took so many volumes to say just that. Of course I go about pretending otherwise, but the fact is, no matter how important the subject I am discussing, let a beautiful woman appear and I know where my brain is. Except when I am seriously gambling. Perhaps, I thought, gambling is to me what socialism is to Font and Levy, but that didn't strike me as true.

'Edna,' I whispered. She moved her head slightly but continued to gaze out of the window. I ran my finger slowly

34

up and down her sleeve. 'Edna . . . Edna . . . Edna . . .' She turned her head and looked at me. For a moment I thought it was a shadow playing on her cheek; at the same instant my hand involuntarily flew to my eyes and covered them. There was silence and then I heard Font and Levy go outside. From the corner of her lips, up her right cheek and to the lobe of her ear, was a thick line of raw flesh. The centre of the line was depressed and of a darker hue than the rest. The stitching had pulled her lips slightly to one side, and part of the skin on her neck was similarly stretched because of the wound.

'Give me a cigarette,' she said very softly. My hands were wet with sweat. I gave her a cigarette, then took one myself and lit both.

'How do you like me now,' she said.

'I love you,' I answered.

'I mean aesthetically.'

A bloody officer. She didn't have to tell me. A bloody bastard of an officer, come to search her house. A dashing swine of an officer with a moustache. Charming at the beginning. 'Just routine,' he must have said. A good lay, someone must have told him . . . a Jewess. What with? A knife? A broken glass?

'A whip,' she said without being asked.

'So what?' I shouted. 'So bloody what? Aren't there bloody officers in Israel? Haven't they massacred Arab women and children? Isn't Kenya full of bloody British officers? Isn't Algeria full of bloody sadists in uniform? So what? Aren't there Jewish officers in filthy Nato hand in hand with ex-Nazi officers? . . . oh, Edna . . . Who was it?'

She didn't answer.

35

'Who was it, Edna?'

But she wouldn't tell.

She looked very much older than myself, and very tired. A storm of affection for her whirled in me, and the uselessness of it all and the unfairness of it all dulled my senses and made me want to cover myself with bedclothes and not open my eyes or emerge for a long time. I tried to pull her towards me, but she pushed me back. I desisted and she sat back, giving me her unscarred side.

All this is London. All this is London I told myself. All this comes of hearing Father Huddleston speak, of knowing who Rosa Luxemburg was, of seeing Gorki's trilogy in Hampstead. It comes of Donald Soper at Speaker's Corner, of reading Koestler and Alan Paton and Doris Lessing and Orwell and Wells and *La Question* and even Kenneth Tynan. Of knowing how Franco came to power and who has befriended him since, of Churchill's hundred million to squash Lenin and then later the telegram; of knowing how Palestine was given to the Jews and why . . . of the bombing of Damascus and Robert Graves's *Good-bye*. Oh, blissful ignorance. Wasn't it nice to go to the Catholic church with my mother before I ever heard of Salazar or of the blessed troops to Ethiopia?

'When did it happen?'

'It doesn't matter,' she answered.

'Where do you live now?'

'A few yards from here.'

'And your parents?'

'In South Africa.'

I stood up and walked about the room. I looked under Font's bed and found a bottle of cognac but I didn't feel

36

like drinking. I looked out of the other window and saw Font and Levy downstairs with the owner of a coffee-house, sitting in chairs on the pavement and playing dominoes, the three of them. Did Font really like to play dominoes, or did the scene of himself and Levy playing with a man in peasant clothes complete a cherished self portrait?

'Do you want some cognac, Edna?'

'Yes,' she answered. I took the bottle from underneath the bed and poured her a glass.

'Why don't you go away, Edna? Why don't you go to Israel or South Africa or France or anywhere else and live and be happy?'

'Because I am Egyptian,' she said.

It took me some time to realize that this scar on Edna's face was actually a disfigurement, and that it affected me as such; not as a repulsiveness, but in the tender way it endeared her to me. Somehow it made her more real and an individual. If only she would cry, I was thinking, if only she would cry and allow her emotions to overcome her thoughts. But in all the six years I had known her, she had never cried.

'Do you ever cry, Edna?' She brushed the question away as stupid.

It is strange. A man gets to know a woman. For a long time they are one. They have mingled their thoughts, their bodies, their hopes, their odours, their lives. They are one. And then a while later they are strangers. They are not one any more. Just as though it had never happened, as though looking at oneself in the mirror and seeing a stranger instead of one's reflection.

I fetched a glass. What do people who do not drink do on such occasions? Face the facts perhaps. But facing a fact is one thing, and overcoming it is another. Cognac was going to overcome the facts: overcome Edna's willed hardness and overcome my lack of suitable words and actions. I filled my glass and hers once more, then sat at her feet in silence, she with her thoughts and I with mine. The cognac was already taking control of things. One more glass each and I kissed her on her knee, softly and affectionately. Slowly her hand came down and played with my hair and rubbed my head against her side. Spontaneous, perhaps, and unpremeditated; nevertheless a scene probably already encountered in a film or a play or an opera or a book which the brandy unknowingly evoked. Artists try to depict people; and people depict the artists' conception of people.

And then the obvious thing to say and talk about came to me: 'Do you remember?' Would I have thought of that if it weren't for the brandy? Perhaps I would have and even did; but it wouldn't have come softly and at the right moment.

'Do you remember?'

'What?' she whispered.

We remembered, and the stranger in the mirror became familiar once more, recognizable and close and one and the same.

Font and Levy came in and ignored the fact that my head was against Edna's knee and her hand on my head. Such irrelevant things are never worthy of the attention of socialists. I was going to ask Font what, in his opinion, Lenin would have done had he discovered his wife with another man, but I changed my mind.

'Everything is Allah's will,' Font began. 'Ask him how much money a year he makes, and he answers: "Allah be praised, enough." Ask him whether he is happy Nasser has rid us of Farouk, he answers: "Whatever God brings is good." Ask him how much he pays his waiter, he says: "Allah knows, more than enough." '

Levy said there was a 'psychological barrier' between Font and Kharafallah downstairs. But Font said he was only a hired hand in the snooker club, and therefore no such barrier should exist, and Edna said something about being careful not to patronize. I waited to see how the conversation would turn to English politicians. If it didn't turn in that direction soon, I was going to steer it that way myself because they are never so happy as when beating the bush in London. However, Edna told Font he was acting like a Fabian, and Levy illustrated Fabianism by describing Bernard Shaw, and Font defended Wells, so they were on the right track and I rubbed my head against Edna's knee.

'I'll drive you home,' I told Edna.

'I live next door,' she said.

'Let's all go for a drive.'

'All right,' she said.

Just as we were going out of the door, Levy turned to Edna and said: *'Tu te sens mieux?'*

I saw her frown slightly; she didn't like this particular intimacy simply because they were both Jewish. At the same time Levy's face reddened at his mistake.

We heard music as we approached the car, and I remembered the little boy who offered to clean it. He was curled up in the front seat, asleep, the rag with which he had cleaned the car still clasped in his hand. We all peered at him as I explained how he came to be there. Edna put the radio off and woke him gently.

'Where do you live?' she asked. He rubbed his eyes and looked at us from under his eyebrows, his head bent. Then he saw me and smiled.

'I've cleaned it *three* times,' he said.

'It's beautiful,' I said.

'Where do you live?' Edna asked again. 'Your mother must be worried about you.'

'Oh, it's all right, mistress,' he said, 'I have no mother or father, so it's all right.'

'Where do you live then?'

'Oh, just here.'

'Which house?'

'In one of the doorways, it doesn't matter which.'

'You mean you have no home?'

'No, but in winter I sleep behind the police officer's desk at the station.'

'Police officer?'

'Yes, he is my friend,' he said proudly. I watched Font's face. I could see the genuine frustration and the anger at his inadequacy and the injustice of it seep up to his eyes and blind him with useless fury.

'How old are you?' Edna asked.

'I don't know.'

Just then Kharafallah, the coffee-house owner, came and peered at the boy. 'No father, no mother,' he sighed. 'What can we do? It's God's will.'

'Where does he eat?' Levy asked.

'Here and there. A loaf here, a bit of cheese there; we do what we can – he is not the only one. What can we do? It's Allah's will.'

'Doesn't he go to school?' Font in his dreaminess asked.

'School? What school? He has no father or mother I tell you.' Kharafallah shook his head. 'School indeed!' He laughed. 'This one is lucky; the police officer, a good man, may God keep him, helps him in the cold. What can we do?'

Edna gave Kharafallah some money and told him to look after the boy until we made some arrangement for him.

We drove towards the Pyramids, Edna and me in the back seat, and Font driving with Levy by his side. Levy had his arms crossed in resignation. He is authentically lonely. We first met him in London, working in a Lyons Corner House, shouted at by an unpleasant manageress. He has never quite fitted in with us. Apart from our having had an English education and he a French one, there is an aura of humility about him which is sometimes embarrassing. Edna paid his passage to Egypt and Font befriended him. He teaches Arabic now to adult Egyptians who have suddenly been faced with the necessity of knowing that language, which he had studied under Moslem Sheikhs at the Azhar University. He would probably have become a scholar of repute in the Arab world had it not been for the Suez war. I wondered why he didn't go to Israel.

'Levy,' I asked, 'have you ever thought of going to Israel?'

'Yes,' he said. 'You can be sure that at one time or another, every Jew has thought of going to Israel.'

I don't know why, but it reminded me of: 'At one time or another every married man has thought of divorce.'

'In the midst of Jews,' he continued, 'I lose all individuality. I agree with everything they say. I act and say whatever they expect of me; I end up by having no thoughts of my own. It would be an act of suicide from my part.'

. . . Un acte de suicide de ma part,

Si je ne me tiens pas à l'écart.

'I'm a poet,' I told them.

We passed the house where my aunt lives and where I met Edna for the first time. I saw her smile slightly. I wondered whether the closeness we had recaptured at Font's had dissipated. I searched for her hand and found it, but there was no response to my caress. I was afraid she would imagine I was feeling sorry for her because of the wound. I *was* feeling sorry, but that had nothing to do with my desire to hold her hand. I loved her.

We drove up to the base of the Pyramids and went out of the car. There they stood. Material monuments of immaterialism. In the darkness they didn't seem man-made, but a godly imposition on this earth, a sign of the stability of some unearthly power. Had they been built much earlier, and had their history been unknown, some Moses or other might well have used them as a sign to some Abraham:

And lo! fire was kindled in the bosom of whoever it was and three earthquakes moved the earth and the waters, and the heavens showered square pillars and filled the earthquakes and behold! built three monuments one by the side of the other: three hundred and three score something or other in height and as many steps as a young lamb will use in one day and one night in breadth. And the fire smouldered in his heart and he bade his five sons to be brought unto him and he smote them and gave orders to sacrifice all the newly wedded on the base of the largest of the monuments. For such was the Lord's wish.

I held Edna's hand and we went off together to see the Sphinx. We stood looking at it in silence for a quarter of an hour, then I turned round and faced her and put my hand on her scarred cheek and told her I loved her. She continued looking at the Sphinx, but I put my mouth on hers and kissed her and held her tight. We walked back to the car, my arm round her waist and hers round mine, like English couples at Brighton.

We drove back in silence. No matter how many times I go to the Pyramids at night, I am always awed, and the return journey is made in silence. We dropped Levy on the way and then Font drove to his rooms. He left the engine running, said good night, and went upstairs. We sat for a while in the back seat without speaking. It had been a long day for me; I had drunk too much and was tired. But I had an overwhelming desire for Edna; a chokingly tender need to caress her and to love her.

'Where do you live?' I asked.

'Come, I'll show you.'

One room, Moorishly furnished with a low sofa on which she slept; but I couldn't see very much because she didn't turn the light on. I knew she wouldn't want lights any more. I sat, Arab fashion, on the sofa and then she came and sat in the same way in front of me. I started to undo her hair as I had often done before, then she handed me a comb and I combed her auburn hair with long, slow sweeps, from her forehead down to her waist; then I plaited her hair and tied the ends with a piece of string she gave me, and undid her clothes and peeled her jacket off, then her blouse and everything else, and she sat in front of me, bare and very beautiful with her head bent. I told her 'I love you' many times, and kissed her, and whispered love and tenderness and memories in her ear. At last she turned round and breathed close

43

to me and we became one. Two bodies and two brains and two lives clasped together, and nothing else mattered. To be loved by, and to possess the person we love is why we were born.

PART II

About six years earlier the aunt who had signed away those acres, was having a reception – a soirée they called it – in honour of her son Mounir, just back from America. It was a large affair in her Pyramid Road villa. Liveried servants, cut glass and champagne. I went late. There were about thirty guests around an enormous table having supper; my chair conspicuously empty.

'And here comes our revolutionary,' Mounir's mother said, 'Nasser's disciple.' A fat, ugly, rich woman. 'Aren't you going to tell them to take our house and silver?' She squeaked in laughter. Everyone else laughed mirthlessly. They were being served by eight servants, permanent staff. I was sitting next to my mother.

'At least say hello to Mounir,' she whispered, 'you haven't seen him for three years.'

I started looking round the table for him. I gave him a glance but my eyes rested on the girl next to him. She had this unique, even, very light brown skin with a mass of auburn hair piled at the back of her head. Her eyelids were moist, I could see that from where I was sitting.

'Who's that?' I asked my mother.

'That's *la fille* Salva, my dear. Just back from Europe.'

Her father and mother were there too; I had met them before. One of the richest Jewish families in Egypt – our Woolworths.

'Long time no see,' shouted Mounir. God, I thought; *Long time no see!*

I looked at him and said hello.

'How's tricks, buddy? Sure will have some fun together soon, eh?' And he winked.

'Tout à fait américain,' someone said, and *'c'est mignon'* and *'il est sympathique.'*

I kept my eyes on my plate, imagining that handsome idiot squirming in his seat. Now and again I gave the Salva girl a look; she always seemed to be smiling at Mounir.

'Hey, Ram,' he shouted to me again, 'what's that I hear about you being Red? Don't fall for that stuff, buddy. I'll give you some information'll make you think.'

I was neither Red, Pink, Blue, nor Black. I had no politics in me then. I didn't consider the Egyptian revolution and getting rid of Farouk to be politics.

'You do that,' I said.

'Believe me,' he continued, and he was speaking to the whole table now, 'American Democracy is *the* thing. Boy, you wanna see that country.' Everyone was nodding at him wisely and contentedly. His American accent, whether intentional or not, added to his insipidness.

'I was there and I saw for myself. Man, that's the country for me. I tell you . . .'

Two days earlier, I had been with a group of 'freedom fighters', all students, harassing the English troops at Suez. Three of my friends had died, and Font was lying in hospital with a bullet in his thigh.

'. . . the Red menace . . . free enterprise . . .' he went on, to the worthless admiration of the nodding seals there. 'We sure must be vigilant,' he said. 'Look what happened to China.'

I asked him what had happened to China. He didn't know. He didn't know there was any racial discrimination in America. He had never heard of Sacco and Vanzetti, he did not know what 'un-American activities' was. No, he did not believe there were poor Puerto Ricans or poor anyone else in America. Who was Paul Robeson? Red Indians without full citizenship? What was I talking about? I must be mad. All he knew was that he had spent three years in America, had picked up their pet phrases and had been given a degree. He was all set to be given high office, and what sickened me was the knowledge that he would get it. It made me sick because apart from Font and myself, all the other students dying at Suez were from poor families and Mounir and Co. were going to lord it over the survivors.

'England,' he said, 'must stay at Suez and protect us from the Red Menace.'

Politics or no politics, that was too much for me. I don't remember what happened exactly; we came to blows and I told him to 'wipe his backside' with his American democracy. Of course my mother started crying, and the servants separated us, and even calling the police was suggested.

I found myself in the street. Strangely, I was in a good mood. I even laughed when I remembered the way my aunt had shouted 'murder, murder'. It was too late for the Pyramid Road tram-line, and I started walking the seven-mile journey home. My mother still had her car then, and I thought she might pick me up later on. I heard my name being called, but walked on without looking back. Then footsteps started running towards me.

'Stop, blast you!' she said.

'What do you want,' I asked, looking at the Salva girl.

'Your mother tells you to take her car; here are the keys.'

'How will she get back?'

'My parents will drive her.'

I started walking back with her.

'I'm the daughter . . .'

'Yes, yes, I know,' I said. 'You're the rich Salva girl.' I started the car.

'Will you drive me home?' she asked.

'Why?'

'Wait a moment,' she said, 'I'll get my handbag.'

She returned a few minutes later and I drove for a while in silence. Suddenly I decided to go and visit Font. He had a private room, and I knew I could enter the hospital any time I wanted.

'You live in Heliopolis, don't you?'

'Yes,' she answered.

I went to our Zamalek flat first and asked her to wait in the car for a moment. Upstairs I collected two bottles of wine and two glasses; then I took another glass.

'Why did you leave the party?' I asked in the car.

'Are you going to seduce me with this wine?' she said, not answering my question. I told her about Font in hospital and that I wanted to tell him about what happened at my aunt's.

'Do you often go to Suez?'

'I don't, but Font is a regular.'

'How old is Font?' she asked.

'Twenty-one.'

'You're twenty-one also?' I nodded.

'I'm twenty-five,' she said.

She came with me to the hospital. No one saw us and we slipped quietly into Font's room. I introduced him to Edna and opened the wine. Edna and I sat at the foot of Font's bed, and I started to tell him about Mounir.

'I was so happy when you hit him,' Edna said.

This surprised me. 'I thought you were smiling at him all the time.'

'I can't stand him or any of the people there.'

'Even your parents?' I asked.

'Particularly them.'

I laughed.

'Why are you laughing?' It was Font who asked.

'A rich girl's gimmick,' I replied.

'No,' she said calmly, 'it isn't.' And I believed her. That was the first time Edna made me ashamed of myself, because I knew that my own behaviour that day was not without the support of some kind of gimmick.

Edna asked Font how he came to be wounded. We talked until dawn. We drank and laughed and were very careful not to mention Israel because Edna was Jewish. My hand accidentally touched hers and somehow it seemed natural that we hold hands for the rest of the night. The wine and the dawn and Edna's beauty made me feel very much in love. It was a happy night.

Font was discharged from hospital soon after that day when Edna and I went to see him. We began to meet Edna nearly every day. Sometimes she'd come and pick us up from the university by car, and we would drive for hours on the desert road to Alexandria. Font and I were shy people, and fundamentally very different from our old school friends – different in spite of sharing their taste for drink and gambling: we were bookworms. Font was living with my mother and myself then. Both his parents were dead and we had been friends since childhood. He had a small monthly allowance which he shared with me for books and expenses, while my mother paid for the household. We hadn't arranged it that way, it just came naturally. We were such avid readers, we sometimes spent weeks on end without going out of my room, reading one book after another. I don't remember ever discussing a book with Font. We just read.

The only important thing which happened to us was the Egyptian revolution. We took to it wholeheartedly and naturally, without any fanaticism or object in view. The only time I was passionate about it was that day when I heard Mounir say the English should remain in Egypt. And, surprisingly, that was also the first time I had ever used my reading: racial discrimination and incidents such as Sacco and Vanzetti, I had come across amongst the thousands of books I consumed. To someone of the opposite type to Mounir I could as well have talked about the murders of Karl Radek and the Polish revolutionaries. I read detachedly and was interested only in the stories as such.

When Edna began talking to us of socialism or freedom or democracy, we always said yes, that's what the Egyptian revolution was; everything good was going to be carried out by the revolution. To begin with Edna's politics were not noticed by us at all, but gently she talked to us about oppressed people in Africa and Asia and even some parts of Europe, and Font and I started to read political books with more interest. The more we read, the more we wanted to learn and the more ignorant we felt. We learnt, for the first time, the history of British imperialism and why we didn't want the British troops in the Suez Canal area. Up to then we had shouted 'evacuation' like everyone else, without precisely knowing why evacuation was so important. Gradually, we began to see ourselves as members of humanity in general and not just as Egyptians.

We started to feel dissatisfied with the university life we were leading. This did not make us work any harder. If we were not playing snooker or drinking beer, we were with Edna, and if neither of these, we were devouring political books.

Edna and I were not lovers straight away. I had met too many Egyptian girls at the university who were vehement politicians and who considered a man's physical approach with contempt, so loving Edna silently, I was afraid that she too would find it contemptible if I tried to make love to her. I started to pour some of my passion into politics. I later learnt that a man who has passion in his politics is usually attractive to women.

It was Edna who introduced me to Egyptian people. It is rare, in the milieu in which I was born, to know Egyptians. She explained to me that the Sporting Club and the race meetings and the villa-owners and the European-dressed and - travelled people I met, were not Egyptians. Cairo and Alexandria were cosmopolitan not so much because they contained foreigners, but because the Egyptian born in them is himself a stranger to his land.

She took me one day to a flat her father owned near old Cairo. It was the first of many trips, bare-foot and in peasant dress, to the poor districts of Cairo and to the little villages in the outskirts. That first day, she made me sit Arab fashion on the floor and told me to comb her hair. She sat in front of me and took some hair-pins out. Her hair fell down to her waist and I combed it and plaited it, then tied the plaits with strings. On the bed were the peasant clothes we were to wear.

'Are you sad?' she asked without turning her head.

'A little bit.' It was that calm sadness which . . . well, which comes over you if you are combing the hair of the woman you love and if you don't feel good enough for her.

'Now we must wear these clothes,' she said without moving.

'Yes,' I said.

'Do you mind if I undress in front of you?'

'Don't, Edna.'

'Why?'

I didn't answer.

'Is it because you love me?'

I stared at the nape of her neck in silence.

'I am four years older than you.'

'Does it matter?'

'No,' she said.

After a while she asked me if I were as naïve as I appeared to be. I bent forward and kissed her neck. 'I am not naïve,' I whispered, 'but I am clumsy because I love you.'

'Say it again,' she said.

'What?'

'That you love me.'

'I love you,' I said.

Unconsciously, all the books we had read, political and otherwise, began to be more than just interesting reading to Font and me. Edna had read nearly as much as we had, and under her influence we began to talk about what we had read.

The world of ice and snow in winter and red, slanting roof-tops was beginning to call us. The world of intellectuals and underground metros and cobbled streets and a green countryside which we had never seen, beckoned to us. The world where students had rooms, and typists for girl-friends, and sang songs and drank beer in large mugs, shouted to us. A whole imaginary world. A mixture of all the cities in Europe; where pubs were confused with zinc bars and where Piccadilly led to the Champs-Elysées; where miners were communists and policemen fascists; where there was something called the 'bourgeoisie' and someone called the 'landlady'; where there were Grand Hotels and Fiat factories and bull-fighting; where Americans were conspicuous and anarchists wore beards and where there was something called the 'Left'; where Christopher Isherwood's German family lived, where the Swedes had the highest standard of living and where poets lived in garrets and there were indoor swimming-pools.

I wanted to live. I read and read and Edna spoke and I wanted to live. I wanted to have affairs with countesses and to fall in love with a barmaid and to be a gigolo and to be a political leader and to win at Monte Carlo and to be down-and-out in London and to be an artist and to be elegant and also to be in rags.

It was the last day before the summer holidays; all the well-to-do were going to Alexandria. Font and I were waiting for Edna near the university gate.

'Here we are,' Font said, 'the beginning of the three months, the crowded beaches and showing-off. All the "family" girls expecting a platonic love affair and all the young men polishing their moustaches and parading on the sea-shore. The gambling and the young men driving their cars and the night-clubs and the boasting about imaginary affairs. The coloured shirts and trousers for the girls. The same old thing and all empty . . . no life.'

I agreed. 'Life' was in Europe.

I don't know whether Edna had made up her mind a long time before, but unexpectedly she came out with a plan to take us to England for three months. I had never been able to penetrate very deeply into her thoughts. Why she befriended Fond and myself and initiated us into politics and was having an affair with me, I could not guess, and at the time did not think about it. Perhaps it was because the three of us had had an English education and spoke in English, perhaps she was lonely, perhaps she considered it her social duty to do all this. She never told me she loved me, and if she had, I would not have believed her. I imagined Edna loving a strong-willed, sober man dedicated to something noble which she respected, and I was very far from being any of these things. Perhaps she liked me because of that incident at my aunt's the first time we met, but she was too intelligent not to see it had been partly an act. Anyhow, she proposed taking us to England at her expense.

Someone wants to travel. If he has no passport, he gets one. He fills an application form, presents his birth-certificate and one or two other papers, and in a few days' time he is given a passport. It is his birthright. It was the passports which started Font off on being puzzled, before he even reached Tilbury. It took us three months and one day to get our passports. For the three months we were on our own, and no amount of papers and excuses and pulling strings

56

and explaining could yield us our passports. Then we met an old friend of ours whose father was well placed in the army. In the one day we obtained two passports simply by giving him two pictures each. He also got us exit-visas in half an hour.

'You'd think we were criminals or something' Font told me, 'imagine needing a visa to *leave* the country. It's disgusting. And then, after three months of useless toil, a man obtains it in half an hour. To think I go and risk my life in Suez every now and then for a country where strings still have to be pulled.'

'Give them time, Font. They've only been a very short time in power.'

'It's not a short time,' he answered. Later, it was Font himself who found excuses for such things. 'Less than one per cent of the population have the urge to, can, or have to leave the country. This democratic sophistry of a right to have a passport is all right in a country where eighty per cent of the population isn't half starving. So what, if this one per cent is restricted?' But that wasn't yet; at this time his 'education' was still at its primary stage.

I wrote a letter from England once, some years later, to someone in Eypt telling him not to send his son to an English school. If his son was one of those who swallowed what they were told, he would one day be disgusted. At school Font and I had been among the very few who 'swallowed'. We said 'this isn't cricket', and didn't smoke with our school blazers on because we had 'promised' not to do so. We had been implanted with an expectation of 'fair play' from the English. This stupid thing of expecting 'fair play' from the English, alongside their far from 'fair play' behaviour, was a strange phenomenon in us. Perhaps in our subsequent outcries against the English, there was the belief that if they *knew* that what they were doing wasn't fair play, they would stop it. In spite of all the books we had read demonstrating the slyness and cruelty of England's foreign policy, it took the Suez war to make us believe it. Of course the Africans and the Asians had had their Suezes a long time before us . . . over and over again. I say this now, because of what happened when we tried to get entry visas for England.

Having obtained our passports and our exit visas, we hurried to the British consulate for our British visas. Egyptians were then travelling to England, and Britons to Egypt, the situation at Suez had eased and there was talk of a settlement. We filled two application forms.

'Which school did you go to?' a clerk asked. We told him.

'You're only going for a visit?'

'That's right.'

He came back ten minutes later and told us he was very sorry, but he couldn't give us our visas.

We went to see the headmaster of the school we had matriculated from. We had been fond of him as a person. He telephoned the consulate and spoke to a friend of his to see why we had been refused visas.

'Good lord, man!' he shouted into the phone, 'that's not a reason for refusing these two young men visas,' then turned round and told us he was very sorry, but that there was nothing he could do. He offered us cigarettes and told us he understood our disappointment. Font said he was more disgusted than disappointed.

The headmaster spoke quietly to us. He told us frankly that it was all a matter of politics. He didn't mince his words. The school was run for rich Arabs and Egyptians who, it was hoped, would later rule in their parents' place. The school was there to see that they ruled in Britain's favour. 'You two are Copts,' he said, 'and as the ruling power is entirely Moslem now, they do not bother to give you visas.' He looked pained.

'Why do you want to go to England?' he asked me.

'I don't know, sir. Nothing in particular. To see what a pub is like perhaps; to walk in Piccadilly and to listen at Speaker's Corner.'

He smiled, then took his headmaster's attitude: 'Go to the Swedish Consulate,' he said authoritatively, 'and apply for a visa to Sweden. Then apply for a transit visa through England. They cannot refuse you that. In the meantime I shall write a letter to someone in England to whom you have to go as soon as you arrive in London.' He wrote down an address and gave it to us. Then he shook hands with both of us and said he hoped we had a pleasant time.

The Swedish Consulate politely gave us visas while we waited and the British Consulate gave us transit visas, making it clear that we were not to remain in the United Kingdom more than ten days. 'I'll stay ten years if I wish, you sly bastard,' Font whispered behind the clerk's back.

Edna was already in Europe, in Switzerland with her parents. She had paid for our passages and was to meet us in London.

We sat up late at night, Font and I, talking in my room. I have had many intimate relationships with both men and women since that period, but nothing has ever been near the relationship we enjoyed then. The mental sophistication of Europe has killed something good and natural in us, killed it for good . . . for ever. To me, now, it is apparent that we have, both Font and myself, lost the best thing we ever had: the gift of our birth, as it were; something indescribable but solid and hidden and, most of all, natural. We have lost it for ever. And those who know what it is, cannot possess it . . . Gradually, I have lost my natural self. I have become a character in a book or in some other feat of the imagination; my own actor in my own theatre; my own spectator in my own improvised play. Both audience and participant in one – a fictitious character.

. . . We left, Font and I, for London. For dreamed-of Europe, for 'civilization', for 'freedom of speech', for 'culture', for 'life'. We left that day and we shall never return, although we are back here again.

We sailed from Port Said to Tilbury. The first thing we did on the ship was to ask for a mild and bitter. It tasted watery but it was mild and bitter and that was enough for us. Then we drank a whole list of other names we knew all about but had never tasted.

I think it was to Euston Station that we went from Tilbury. Edna stood there, smart and very beautiful, waiting for us. I don't remember much except that the three of us were happy and that Font and I were full of gratitude to Edna. Just to stand in the streets of London was satisfaction enough for us.

We stayed at an hotel near Hyde Park Corner. The second day of our arrival we wrote to Dr Dungate, the man whose address had been given us by our old headmaster, and promptly received an answer asking us both to spend Sunday with him and his family in their house in Hampstead.

Edna was good enough not to talk politics during those first days. The only thing she did was to introduce us to the *New Statesman* and *The Guardian*. We went to the theatres and twice to the Houses of Parliament. As I have said, I never thought Edna was in love with me, and during those first days in London, I was sure she wasn't. I was too dependent on her. I followed her too meekly for her to feel anything but affection and friendliness towards me. A woman will never fall in love with a man who does not dominate her, however slightly. She took me as her lover sometimes and I was wise enough not to show her how much I loved her. Perhaps it was this fact of my not manifesting my love which attracted her to me; it introduced an element of mystery in our relationship. Women sometimes confuse curiosity with love.

On Sunday, Font and I decided we wouldn't go empty-handed to Dr Dungate.

'Don't be stupid,' Edna said, 'you don't have to take anything. You're in England now, not in Egypt.'

We agreed, but bought flowers on the way all the same. We were still natural. If it was not in our nature to go empty-handed, we didn't. If someone had told us, 'don't be so damned Oriental in your ways,' we would have been perplexed to think we could be anything else but that.

Contentedly standing in a queue, we waited for a bus in Park Lane.

'Two sixpences,' Font said. We liked to say 'two sixpences' and 'two fours' and 'three twos', it was London to us.

' 'Ere you are, luv.'

'Ta,' said Font.

Most passengers alighted at Marble Arch and we were the only ones on the top. The conductress stood behind us; a small woman in her forties.

'Oo's the lucky girl?' she asked, pointing to the flowers.

'As a matter of fact, they're for a man,' I said.

'Gaw on!' she teased.

'Well, they're for a family.'

'Flowers are ever so nice, they are. Nothin' so cheerful as 'avin' 'em at home. I'm sure they'll be ever so pleased with them.'

'Thank you,' I said.

She went forward and tapped the 'all clear' signal with her foot.

'You're not English, are you, luv?'

'No,' I said, 'we're Egyptian.'

'Egyptian! Fancy that now. D'you like it 'ere, luv?'

'Yes, very much.'

'Fancy you being Egyptian and my Steve just back from . . . now wot's the name of that place . . .'

'Suez,' Font said.

'That's right, Suez. Ever so 'appy 'e was there 'e said. As dark as an Indian 'e came back, wot with the swimming and the sun. Beautiful place 'e said it was.'

'I'm glad he liked it,' Font said.

' 'Ere,' she said, 'you come an' 'ave a cup of tea with us next week. Steve'll be ever so pleased to meet you, I'm sure.'

'Thank you,' we both said.

'Steve said as 'ow 'e never got to know the natives there, wot with army rules and all that. I'm sure 'e'll be ever so pleased to meet you.'

'Thank you,' we said.

'You been long 'ere, luv?'

'About a week.'

'It's cold for you I 'xpect. You want to be careful, dears, and wear something warm next to your skins. You want to keep your bodies nice and warm 'ere, luv. That's our house there, number twelve. Now you be sure and come on Saturday, then we can nip round the corner and 'ave a Guinness,' she winked. Her name was Mrs Ward. She wrote her address on the back of a ticket and ran downstairs. We got off at West Hampstead and waved to her.

We walked in silence to Hampstead via Swiss Cottage. The double-deckers and the slanting roof-tops and the pubs and the Underground stations were all there. We walked and watched and felt the little hustle of people at Hampstead station penetrate to us. Hampstead was more England than Knightsbridge.

Dr Dungate lived in a semi-detached house up a narrow, sloping street. We pressed the bell and waited. Somehow I expected the exact replica of our old headmaster to open the door.

'Do you think a butler opens the door?' Font asked.

'Of course,' I answered. 'Jeeves himself will *usher* us in and announce our names in perfect Arabic and ask if we would like an ouzo or whatever we Egyptians are supposed to drink.'

Instead, there was a buzz and the door opened by itself.

'Come in, come in, young men,' a voice shouted from the top of the stairs. 'Hang your coats and come up. Was it difficult finding your way?'

'No, sir,' we shouted, just like schoolboys. We hung up our overcoats and went upstairs. There was a very tall man, stooping under his length, waiting at the top. He wore an old tweed jacket, tight and too short at the back, with leather protection at the elbows.

'Now which of you is Ram and which is Font?' he asked.

'I am Font, sir,' said Font, 'but I am surprised you know that name; it's only a nickname.'

Dr Dungate laughed. 'Ha,' he said, 'I have a little biography of you two, here.'

He heartily shook hands with us.

'You are very welcome here,' he said, 'and we don't want you to feel in the least bit strangers. Come and meet the family. Ha,' he said, looking at the flowers. 'That's very nice of you. That's for Mother I expect; she's in the kitchen and we'll visit her in due course. But here, first, is my son and my daughters.'

He had three daughters in their twenties and a thirty-year-old son who looked like his father. 'That's Jean, that's Barbara, that's Brenda and that's my son John.' We all shook hands and they said 'hello, Ram' and 'hello, Font'.

'Now come and meet Mother. We're having a typical Sunday meal for you, and Mother is making sure it is one of her best.'

We followed him to the kitchen. He put a hand each on our shoulders and sort of gave us to his wife.

'Here they are, Mother.'

She was also tall and rather thin, with a lively look in her bright blue eyes.

'What lovely flowers,' she said, wiping her hands; 'it's very nice of you to have thought of that.' She shook hands with us and told us we were both welcome.

We went back to the sitting-room and sat, rather shy, with our arms crossed, answering questions. Our old headmaster turned out to be Mrs Dungate's brother, and we were told he had always loved Egyptians, 'but unfortunately he is having trouble reconciling his views with those of the governing body of the school'. Dr Dungate was reading the letter to him about us.

'Ah,' he said, skipping a page, 'we have this spot of bother about the visas. I cannot promise you anything and I do not want you to be disappointed, so I shall not give you any high hopes. You must bear in mind that if you are refused an extension of your stay, you must make sure you leave by the specified date.' He lowered the letter and looked at us from above his spectacles by bending his head. There was both amusement and severity in his look. Mrs Dungate stood at the doorway listening.

'If I were you I wouldn't leave . . . if you want to stay, that is.' It was John who said that.

'Now don't put any foolish ideas in their heads, John,' his mother said. 'I'm sure we'll do all we can to have them stay, but they must not do anything against the law.'

'I suppose you call eighty thousand of our soldiers in Suez against Egyptian wishes, not against the law?' he said, standing up and walking about, his hands deep in his pockets.

'Please, John.'

'I'm sure every one of them has a visa duly stamped and paid for at the Egyptian consulate, otherwise they wouldn't be in Suez. We English never break the law,' he said; 'it's so malleable in our capable hands.'

'We'll jolly well see you stay,' one of the girls said.

'Now, now,' Dr Dungate said, 'we shall discuss the possibilities calmly, and see which is the best way of going about it. I am going to ask a Labour Member of Parliament I know to . . .'

'Labour M.P.!' pooh-poohed John. 'Dad, you always refuse to see the true colours of most of those Labour M.Ps. Have you forgotten Sere . . . ?'

'I can hardly ask the Communist Party to help them, can I?' his father said. John thrust his hands deeper in his pockets and sat down.

Did Englishmen really rage against their own injustices? Font, his eyebrows reaching a good zenith of height, was staring at John with all his might.

'I don't think you would ask the Communist Party even if they could help,' Brenda said. Brenda was the youngest and somehow different from her sisters. She wore a plain, neat dress and was simply combed, whereas Jean and Barbara wore trousers and had their hair in pony tails; which didn't suit the eldest, Barbara, at all.

Dr Dungate looked at us apologetically and smiled.

'We have four different political opinions in this house,' he said, 'and I am supposed to be wholeheartedly in support of each one of them. John belonged to the Communist Party until recently, but is now disillusioned. Brenda is a communist and was selling the *Daily Worker* at eight o'clock this morning. My wife is simply liberal, and my two other daughters vote Labour. We have four daily papers in the house: *The Guardian*, the *Daily Herald*, the *Daily Worker*, and four weeklies; the . . .'

'You forgot *The Times*, Dad,' John said.

'Yes, and *The Times*.'

Jean was interested in Font. She had a lazy, comfortable look about her and politics didn't interest her.

'Dad,' she said, 'I'm sure we're boring Font and Ram with all this.'

'Not at all,' we said.

'Well, I'm for a pint before lunch,' she said. 'Who's coming with me?'

No one answered.

'Come on, Font; you and I'll have a pint together and you can talk to me about the Nile and the Pyramids.' She caught his hand and pulled him up. I wanted to drink too, were it only to shake me out of this lethargy of gratitude and shyness.

'We'll all go for a pint,' John said. 'Come on, Mummy.'

'No, dear. I can't go and I don't want your father to drink today; he has to work this afternoon and it will only make him sleepy.'

'But I'm taking Font to another pub,' Jean said, 'I don't want to listen to any more of your politics.'

'Font, you've 'ad it, she taykin' a fancy ter yer.'

Font laughed embarrassedly.

'I'm going to seduce you, Font,' Jean said. 'Don't you love me a teeny-weeny bit?'

'I love you all,' he said.

'Isn't that sweet,' Mrs Dungate said. 'Now off all of

you and don't drink too much. Lunch at two o'clock.'

We all went downstairs, putting scarfs and coats on and the girls using their mirrors. There is a certain solitude when a group of people is preparing to go out, which I always relish after sitting in tension at meeting new people and being rather tongue-tied. It is like leaving a party in full swing and going to the seclusion of the toilet for a few minutes with the receding noise to accentuate the privacy. I put my coat on slowly and wondered whether meeting these people and receiving their hospitality was really enjoyable. That moment of putting on my coat was the very beginning – the first time in my life that I had felt myself cleave into two entities, the one participating and the other watching and judging. But the cleavage was not complete then, the two forces had only just started to pull in different directions.

Jean and Font went off to a different pub and said they would join us later.

'That's where I live,' Barbara said, pointing to a window on the way to the pub.

'Don't you live with your parents?'

'No; Brenda is the only one living with them. John lives in Baker Street and Jean lives in Swiss Cottage.' This puzzled me. Dr Dungate's house seemed large enough to house them all.

We all drank beer in pints. Edna had already explained that if I were offered a beer in England, I must buy a round later on. I enjoyed carrying the glasses to the bar and saying: 'Four pints of bitter, please.'

'Brenda,' I asked, 'are you really a member of the Communist Party?'

'Really?' she smiled. 'Yes, I am. I have been since I was fifteen.'

'What do you think of Nasser?'

'Here's to Nasser,' she said and drank her beer.

'And yet,' I said, 'he imprisons communists.'

'Yes,' John said, 'how can you drink to the health of someone who imprisons communists?'

She didn't hesitate: 'I drink to anyone who deals imperialism a blow.'

'That's typical! That's why I left the Party. Harry Pollit tells you to support Nasser, so you do.'

'John dear, I know precisely why you left the Party.' She possessed a type of calm reminiscent of Edna.

'I gave the correct reason for leaving the Party.'

'Correct, but not true.'

'Ha! You make a difference between correct and true? Exactly why I left the Party. The "correct" tactics and propaganda had nothing to do with the truth.'

I was enjoying myself. Not particularly because of what we were talking about, but because I was there in a pub with the 'intellectuals' I had read about in books, and because the girls were attractive, and because John was such a likeable person. It was natural to want to fit this environment to the books I had read, and to tell myself: here you are, Ram . . . 'life'.

Barbara told John she wished he'd go back to the Party and put a stop to all this bickering between him and Brenda. But they continued talking about the coming elections and whether the communists should vote Labour. The argument grew heated and even Barbara joined in.

I was just over seventeen when I voted for the first and only time in my life. With my thumb. What I mean is, I pressed my thumb, voluntarily, on an inky pad and then pressed it again, where I was told, on a space next to a name. A boy called Kamal had said: '*Tu veux faire la noce ce soir?*' I had nodded. 'Come over then; best Scotch *et puis on paye un petit poucet,*' I didn't know what '*payer un petit poucet*' meant, but I pretended that I did.

I was at the university then. At last the monotony of school life had ended. The university: strikes, fighting policemen, shouting slogans, stealing sulphur and nitrates from the lab; life at last. And besides, I was in the best of the best – the faculty of medicine. No matter, of course, that my Arabic was deplorable, and that I was, according to a certain Oxford and Cambridge Examination Board, proficient in literature and mathematics but certainly not in biology. No matter that hundreds of much better qualified people queued to be accepted by the faculty. I was one of the privileged; I had strings to pull. Not that I bothered to pull them; my mother, or one of my aunts, must have pulled one from the dangling assortment within her reach. I became: '*Il fait la médecine, ma chère.*'

We killed a certain Zaki Bey. I don't remember who was in power then, I think Nokrashi Pasha, but I know Zaki Bey was head of the police and he came, together with fifty half-starved policemen, to the faculty of medicine. They had a dilapidated tank with them. After a lot of mechanical repairs and consultations, the tank's gun was pointed at us who were on the roof of the faculty's building, and an explosion took place. Some of us extended our hands, trying to catch whatever was emitted from the tank; but it never reached our outstretched hands. It fell, instead, with a thud, on a car belonging to my aunt which I had borrowed that day without permission. This made me very angry indeed. My aunt was bound to know I had taken the car, considering there was now a hole in its roof. I therefore helped catapult a bomb which had just been manufactured on the roof, and Zaki Bey died.

I don't remember which party I voted for, but we were given whisky and salted pea-nuts, after which we were taken in Cadillacs to vote with our thumbs. (Apart from Kamal, none of us was of voting age.)·

It was only when I went home that I learnt why Zaki Bey had died. He had ordered the Kasr-el-Nil bridge to be opened while a student demonstration was crossing it, causing death to six. A handsome funeral march, comprising half the police force and thousands of civilians was organized for him next day. Photographs of the procession were mournfully published in all the evening papers. Among the civilians in the photographs I noticed the presence of a few future brilliant scientists, including Kamal. They were the ones who had manufactured the bomb on the roof of the faculty of medicine the day before.

The usual two-months' closing of the faculty was ordered and most of us went to the beaches of Alexandria.

The university reopened and again I had to choose a political party to belong to. Roughly, there were the following: the Wafd, the Ikhwan (Moslem Brotherhood), the Communists, and the anti-Wafd.

The Wafd paid well provided you were a good orator and organizer of strikes. They gave you a car and, I was told, free drinks at the Arizona or the Auberge – I forget which.

The Ikhwan was a fearsome thing to belong to. You could be ordered to shoot anyone at any time in cold blood; they paid you with promises both earthly and otherwise, and you had to be active even when the university was closed (as a Copt, I would not have been able to join that one anyhow). The Communists were the respectable though secretive ones; the hard-working, the intelligent, the quiet. No rewards, only risk of imprisonment and misery to the family. The anti-Wafd was the most popular, and was joined by socialists, anarchists, university-closing fans, semi-idealists, progressives, and most of the middle class.

I didn't join any party, but contented myself with being devoted to 'evacuation' and was always the first home whenever a strike was suggested as a blow to British imperialism.

Kamal came to the lab one afternoon wearing a three-weeks' beard, which meant that he had become a member of the Ikhwan.

'Infidel,' he said, 'can you steal the chemistry storeroom's key today?'

I replied that my examinations were next day and that anyhow I would have nothing to do with the Ikhwan. He said that although he had recently joined the Ikhwan, this was a job for the last party to which he had belonged. He then wrote down seven examination questions, telling me to expect them in next day's paper. I started to tell him that I didn't need the questions, thank you very much, then I gave a bit of a start; the questions he gave me were all very different from those I had bought for twenty-five pounds the day before. Furthermore, it would have taken me at least three days to prepare the answers to the questions he had just given me. A mistake, it seemed, had been made. Rewards had been given to the wrong students.

Next morning I walked rather dejectedly to the examination hall; I would barely be able to answer three out of the seven questions. I was greeted with the news that the examination hall had been burnt down and that examinations would be postponed for ten days at least.

Kamal's picture next appeared in the procession consequent to the killing of Nokrashi Pasha, and also in that following the killing of Sheikh-el-Banna, head of the Ikhwan. Just before the revolution Kamal owned two cars, a villa on the Pyramid Road, and a flat in town. I met him once after the revolution. He was riding a number six tram to Shubra, a handkerchief round his neck to protect his collar, wearing an old brown suit and brown plimsolls.

'My market has been closed,' he said sadly after a flowery greeting. 'You infidel,' he added with a smile.

Font and Jean came back from the pub they had chosen. I asked Font whether he remember Kamal.

'Which Kamal?'

'Kamal Hassan.'

'Kamal Hassan? . . . oh, Kamal Hassan in our first university year. Yes; what, is he here?'

'No, no. I was thinking of him.' But Font appeared worried and wasn't paying much attention.

'What's the matter, Font?' We were walking behind the others on our way back to the Dungates' house.

'Nothing.'

'Jesus, Font; here we are, London and everything. What's the matter?'

73

'Nothing.'

'You look so perplexed.' We walked for a while in silence.

'You know, Ram, that wound I received from a bloody Englishman in Suez?'

'Yes.'

'Jean was telling me how good the English really are and that I shouldn't listen to what people – or "foreigners" – said. So I showed her my scar and told her how I got it.

'Well?'

'She said she was very sorry I had been wounded, and then told me her cousin, a girl, had been caught and raped by several Egyptians in Suez and her body was found naked near a stream.'

'Well?'

'Well? Isn't it enough for you?'

'What are you talking about, Font?'

'Isn't it horrible we can do such things?'

'*We?* Have you gone mad, Font? What damned business was it of hers being there when she knew quite well she wasn't wanted?'

'There is a difference between harassing the British troops at Suez and murdering a woman.'

I didn't see why Font wanted to spoil a nice day with such things.

'It's a wonder they're so hospitable to us after what happened,' he said.

'After what happened?'

'Their cousin murdered.'

'A wonder? It's a wonder *we* speak to them at all.' I was getting a bit angry with Font. 'Have you forgotten all those

74

who died while with us in Suez? I suppose you are all set to becoming something like my cousin Mounir.'

'No, no. Don't be stupid, but . . .'

The others waited for us to catch them up so we stopped talking. But for the first time a rift had appeared between Font and me.

We left after lunch. John had talked to me for an hour on how to try for an extension of our stay, and Font was to go drinking with Jean later in the evening.

'Well, Font, what do you think?' What Font thought was, that if in the next election the Labour Party came into power, there wouldn't be any more trouble in Suez.

'I don't mean that, Font. I mean today and meeting the Dungates and all that.'

'I think we should read the *New Statesman* with more attention. It *does* reflect the views of many . . .'

'For Christ's sake, Font. I'm not talking politics. Just being there and going to the pub and the lunch and all that.'

'Jean was telling me Mr Bevan often goes to their house.' I didn't speak any more until we reached the hotel.

'What about Jean?'

'She's nice; but I've taykin' a fancy ter Brenda.'

I went to Edna's room and lay on her bed. I put my hands behind my head and closed my eyes. I saw myself in a large pub, a pint in my hand, giving a speech to hundreds of Johns and Jeans and Brendas. It was a beautiful speech full of witticisms and quotations, telling them all about the cruelty and the misery the English have inflicted upon the millions; and my passion rose so much that I push my pint away untouched, and all their faces were watching, intent and ashamed. And, after a fiery condemnation of their acts,

I said: the English are a race apart. No Englishman is low enough to have scruples, no Englishman is high enough to be free from their tyranny. But every Englishman is born with a certain power. When he wants a thing, he never tells himself he wants it. He waits until there comes to his mind, no one knows how, a burning conviction that it is his moral and religious duty to conquer those who possess the thing he wants . . . and then he grabs it. He is never at a loss for an effective moral attitude to take. When he wants a new market for his adulterated goods, he sends a missionary to teach the natives the gospel of peace. The natives kill the missionary, the Englishman flies to arms in defence of Christianity, fights for it, conquers for it, and takes the market as a reward from heaven.

This speech wasn't Bernard Shaw, but my own spontaneous composition. And at the end there was a colossal silence and then a phenomenal ovation with tears in some eyes and all the women begging me to be their lover. But I walked away, disgusted and lonely in the misty night with the burden of all injustice weighing on my heart. But no sooner had I reached my squalid and dingy room, than Edna was there, rushing into my arms full of love, telling me she had listened to my speech.

The door opened. Edna came in, and sat on the bed.

'How is your visa, Ram?'

'Quite well, thank you, how is yours?'

'I never have trouble with visas.'

'Why not?'

'My father is very rich.'

'No; it's because you're Jewish.'

'Perhaps.'

'Is an Egyptian Jew ever refused a visa to France or to England?'

'No, I suppose not.'

'You know why?'

'Why?'

I pulled a book from under the bed, written by someone in the British military hierarchy: 'Furthermore, the Jewish colony in Egypt would support any attempt to re-occupy the country'. He gave this as an additional reason for the occupation of Egypt.

'I haven't brought you here to pick up racial prejudice,' she said.

The 'haven't brought you here' didn't penetrate for a while.

'Turn to page sixty,' I said. 'You'll find: "And, no doubt, the Coptic population would more than welcome it."'

'There are thousands of such stupid books,' she said.

'I haven't brought you here' I remembered. In ordinary circumstances I wouldn't have thought about it. But today was different. I was acquiring a taste for analysis.

'Why did you bring us here?'

'Because you have been raving about coming to England for a whole year.'

'Europe,' I said.

'Europe, then. Don't worry, you'll see much more of it before you return.'

'Certainly.'

'Good,' she said, after a slight hesitation. 'Perhaps you should make the most of your next days here. You may have to leave soon.'

'Oh, no,' I said. 'I can manage to stay if I want. I can also pull strings if I wish.'

'Really?' she said, standing up. 'This is not Egypt, you know.'

'You'd be surprised,' I said. I could see myself being nasty. It was a new thing to me. To be naturally angry was not new; but to be deliberately nasty was a new sensation.

'What's the matter, Ram?'

Having met what I took to be intellectuals, I was now going to use some of their jargon.

'I'm fed up with being patronized,' I said.

She was hanging her coat up as I said that. I saw her stand still for a moment. Then she hung her coat and came back to the side of the bed.

'I am sorry, Ram. It is true. I am patronizing you both. I didn't imagine you would pay any attention to such things.' She made me feel cheap again; the second time since I said 'a rich girl's gimmick' the first night we met.

'Why not?' I asked.

She hesitated, then said she couldn't explain why.

'Are you angry?' she asked.

I didn't answer. She took her comb out of her handbag and gave it to me. To comb her hair was becoming a sexual fetish between us.

It was strange, to me, that being nasty had paid a reward. She loved me that afternoon. Is there anything more wonderful in this world than to possess the woman you love in the afternoon and after a sleep, to bath and dress and go out hand in hand?

We took the Underground to Aldgate and walked in Commercial Road, looking for the W. W. Jacobs' people.

'How can an Egyptian,' I asked Edna, 'who loves W. W. Jacobs be refused permission to stay in England?'

She kissed me and said Font and I had read more books than was good for us.

Font didn't return that night. He came at eight o'clock in the morning.

' 'Allo, 'allo, 'allo,' I said; 'wot 'ave you been hup to, lad? Ah wouldn't 'ave thought yer capable ov it.' Which was a mixture of Cockney and North Country to me. I was pleased that morning. Edna had been passionate at night and I felt she was on the verge of loving me.

'I am an' all, you know.'

'With Jean?'

'I'm a bit ashamed, Ram.'

'You haven't *raped* her, have you?'

'I wish you wouldn't use that word. I mean being offered such hospitality at her father's and then sleeping with her.'

'Ho ho ho . . . ha ha ha. You're nothing but a backward fellah. Edna,' I shouted across the bathroom, 'come and listen to this.'

She came barefoot in her nightdress and jumped into Font's empty bed.

'What?'

I told her.

'Sweet Font,' she said. 'It is you I should love. You haven't abused them at all . . . she did *want* you?'

Font blushed.

Sweet Font.

The maid suddenly came in and said: 'Oo, 'xcuse me.'

'Not at all, luv,' I said. 'Come in, we're one short.'

She went out saying, 'goings on', and then said 'wogs'

which angered Font and Edna but made me burst out laughing.

'You've changed, Ram,' Font said.

John Dungate had given us a list of things to do about our visas. He had telephoned a friend of his who had something to do with the Home Office.

When we had left Egypt, it had been to all intents and purposes, for three months only. Why I did what I did just before leaving, I don't know. I took my school and university certificates and shoved them in the bottom of my suitcase.

'Font,' I said, 'by some fluke, I have my certificates here which are going to be very useful today. You don't, by any chance, have yours here, too?'

He looked at me for a while in silence.

'Yes, Ram, by a similar fluke, I also have mine here.'

'Font, we *are* leaving at the end of the three months.'

'Don't be a hypocrite,' he said.

Edna was waiting downstairs. We went to the Home Office – Aliens Department – the first of many humiliating and nasty interviews. If ever we felt we were getting too fond of the English, all we had to do was to go to the Aliens Department and dissipate all our illusions.

We waited two hours for our turn, and when we finally did reach a polite clerk it was only to explain what we wanted, be given a number, and wait for another hour or so. Coming from Egypt, we couldn't complain of waiting. It was the expression of the fifty or so people waiting with us which affected us. They were mostly Persians, Irakis, Greeks and Italians. We were not, we felt, in a government department or even a police station; this was an institution, something Kafkaesque in essence, where, for no reason at all, Almighty God waited to penetrate into your brains and desires, prove your inferiority, and shred you to pieces. It was the pleading expression on the faces there which affected us. We spoke to a Greek and to an Iraki. It was the Greek's third time there in two weeks. He was emigrating to Australia, but his papers hadn't come through to Australia House yet. They always refused to extend his visa more than a few days at a time and each time he was told not to expect a further extension. 'I have money,' he said, 'what for I cannot stay one month?' The Iraki was in the London School of Economics. For six months his parents had been sending him fifteen pounds a month instead of thirty. The Home Office considered this inadequate for his needs and was therefore refusing to extend his visa or permit him some part-time job. 'I have been here three years,' he said, 'and have letters from all my professors saying I am an excellent student. But all to no avail.' I was getting depressed listening to them.

Our number was called, and we were led to a long corridor lined with many doors. We waited outside one of them.

'Come in,' someone drawled.

We went in and said 'good morning' to a young man of thirty or so stretched comfortably behind a desk.

'Well?'

'We have a transit visa, and . . .'

'That's enough. If you have a transit visa we allow you to stay here for ten days. If you are a day or two late in leaving, it doesn't matter.'

'But . . .'

'I am not going to have any more discussion. Please leave the room.'

I pulled Font out quickly before he said anything. Outside I told Edna what had happened and we went straight to a pub. Font wanted to leave the country that very day.

'I have a confession to make,' I told Font. 'John's lawyer friend advised against going to the Home Office; he said it was staffed with the rudest people on earth. But I took you there on my own initiative.'

'No, Font,' Edna said, 'it was I asked Ram to go to the Home Office.'

That was true. The evening before I had told Edna we were not to go to the Home Office, but would send our passports by post in which case they would remain there at least three weeks, thus giving us three more weeks in England whether they granted us visas or not. But she begged me to go. 'It is part of your cherished England, you ought to know it,' she had said.

'I am glad we came,' Font said.

That afternoon, Font and I went to one of the London polytechnics and, with the help of our certificates, enrolled for a full-time course and paid one term's fee each. We then wrote a polite note to the Under Secretary of State, enclosed our passports and a certificate from the polytechnic, and posted the lot. Four days later we received a chit allowing us to remain in the United Kingdom until the matter had been considered.

Saturday afternoon we remembered our bus conductress

and her Steve. Edna wanted to come with us. For no apparent reason, we decided to pass her as my sister.

It was sunny and we walked; Edna between Font and myself, holding our arms. Up Park Lane to Marble Arch and on to Kilburn through Edgware Road. I had become a bit 'loud' lately, a sort of cocksureness which I loathed to see in others and yet was aware of in myself. I suppose if a young man feels he is loved by a rich and beautiful woman, it isn't unnatural for him to be a bit arrogant, but my arrogance was not natural. I sincerely believed that if I manifested humility and a loving gratitude to Edna, I would not be loved in return. It is all right for people to pretend that love breeds love, but it is not so. The seed of love is indifference.

In Kilburn, Edna told us, a lot of Irish people lived. All I thought of when she said Irish was 'Black and Tan' which led me to think of boot polish. We could walk for hours, the three of us, without speaking, and then a conversation would spring up effortlessly and die down consumed, naturally and peacefully. Perhaps this was because there was no drama between the three of us. I wondered why, considering I loved Edna, I didn't sometimes prefer to be alone with her; but I don't think either she or myself ever wished that Font was not with us. It was natural and complete for the three of us to be together. Later, when I started to indulge in ultra-sophisticated literature, I learnt that I had a father-fixation or complex or image or whatever you want to call it, towards Font; that Edna had a mother one towards us both, and that consequently she felt guilty because she didn't love both of us in the same way. The rubbish Europeans wallow in sometimes. (Although I didn't think it was rubbish then, but on the contrary was very much impressed.)

We rang Mrs Ward's bell. She lived in a basement with her son Steve. It was very cosy in her sitting-room. There was a little fire in the grate, an old radio, and many old carpets and different, comfortable, shabby armchairs concentrated in the fire's glow, with greasy old books and pictures arranged haphazardly but intimately on bookshelves over the fireplace and on either side of it.

'I'm ever so pleased you came, dears, and it's ever so nice you brought your sister along. I was telling Steve 'ere you must have forgotten all about me. But 'ere you are and ever so pleased we are you came I'm sure.'

We had seen many Steves before – hundreds and hundreds of Steves during the war: ginger hair, a prominent, straight nose and bright blue eyes, with freckles on his face. I thought he looked strange in civilian clothes.

'Pleased to meet you,' he said. He took our coats and gave Edna the best armchair and tried to make us comfortable.

'It's so nice and cosy here,' Edna said.

'Thank you, dear; I do try and make it homely. There's nothin' like a fire at home.'

I wondered why we hadn't thought of bringing Mrs Ward flowers. Perhaps there was a subconscious reason for it. I had already started thinking along these lines.

'How long were you in Suez?' Font asked Steve.

'I was in Aden first, see? Spot of trouble there . . . soon put a stop to *that*. Then to Suez for a couple of months; then to Cyprus for a bit of action – nothing much mind you – then back to Suez for four months.'

'Have you finished with the army?'

'I like the life, mind you; makes a man of you. But five years is enough and I've got Ma to think of; and I'm going steady like . . . hope to get married soon.'

'I do 'ope you like a cup-a-tea, dears,' Mrs Ward said. 'It's ever so nice in this cold weather. But Steve said 'ow it's coffee you drink in these parts and he's bought some for you.'

We said we preferred tea, thank you very much, and she told Steve to see if the kettle was boiling.

'Right-o, Ma,' he said.

'We'll go an' 'ave a beer later on,' she said, winking at us.

During tea we listened to Steve talking about life in Suez. He came out with such things as: 'The natives'll fleece you if you're not careful,' and 'not safe after dark . . . you know what the wogs are like.' He was giving us information he considered useful; in fact he was telling us to be careful when there. It never for an instant occurred to him we were the very natives he was talking about. Dirty Arabs and wogs were as much a menace to us as they had been to his beloved regiment. While he spoke, he was most attentive to us, pouring us tea and offering us cakes and lighting our cigarettes.

His girl friend Shirley came while we were having tea. She was not pretty but attractive in a smart way. Her breasts pointed a tight green pullover and she wore fine stockings and high heels. She, too, said 'pleased to meet you' and had a cup of tea with us.

Edna helped clear the table and, together with Shirley, washed up in the kitchen. Mrs Ward sat comfortably in her armchair, cosy and happy. This world of washing-up and clearing the table hadn't yet reached Font and me. We thanked Mrs Ward for the tea.

'That's all right, dears.'

We all went to the pub, Font with Mrs Ward in front, Steve walking with Edna, and myself with Shirley behind them. In the pub were two men playing chess. One of them talked to Shirley and then asked me whether I played.

'Yes,' I said. I was eager to leave the others. However 'sweet' and 'nice' and kind they were, I was getting bored and now that I had started to cleave into two, one half had started telling the other the truth. The chess player was Shirley's brother, Vincent. He nodded to the others but no more. His partner left the game and I took his place. We started a new game. Half-way through the game we had already drunk three pints of beer each and it was time to speak. Perhaps I have an obsession about drink. I must have such an obsession . . . I feel people are hindered without drink. I don't for a moment doubt that without the beer Vincent and I would not have had this urge to speak. If we hadn't drunk, we might have done no more than play chess, and have parted with only a superficial contact, and all that followed would not have happened.

We lit cigarettes and ignored the chess for a while. First the preliminaries, like runners warming themselves before a race, trying this shoe and that, taking a pullover off – one skin less before the race: how long had I been in England and how long was I going to remain, and what was his job, and did he like it. This over, we prodded each other deeper. The Egyptians he had met he didn't like – all they cared for was a good time. He supposed I was 'pretty well off' coming all that way for a holiday. Was he sneering? It didn't matter.

My watching half approved of the dialogue as an opening scene. But apart from that, I felt instinctively that he was more real than John Dungate. I knew that with the Dungates I could have said any old stupid thing and they would have pretended interest and would certainly not have sneered. And then suddenly, I became aware that I was judging the English, first as English and then as human beings. Vincent was essentially free from any racial traits. He was neither a 'Left' Englishman, nor one who was anti-Left, neither a public-school one, nor an L.C.C. one, neither an Anglo-Indian one nor a 'living in Spain' one. He was Vincent Murphy and no more. (He turned out to be the only one amongst all those I met in England who continued to be my friend when I was penniless and in trouble.)

Edna made me a sign I should join the others. I ignored her. I was beginning to know what I felt like doing, and to do it, even if, as a result, I was rude. And, I thought, the more I did that, the more Edna would be attracted to me.

'No,' I told Vincent, 'I'm not well off. As a matter of fact I, personally, am penniless. But I have very rich aunts and uncles and cousins and, anyway, this trip is being paid for by . . . actually by a very rich Jew, although I don't think he knows it.'

'You're well off,' he said, 'rich relatives . . . expensive clothes . . . you're well off.'

'So I'm well off, so what?'

'Oh nothing. It's your move.'

'No,' I said, 'I'm well off; go on from there.'

He looked at me for a while with what I took to be a con-descending smile.

'Most of your people are starving there,' he said. 'Ever hear of the fellah?'

'That's right,' I said. 'They *are* half starving. Isn't is bloody horrible my relatives are wallowing in wealth?'

'It *is*,' he sneered.

'Yes, it is,' I repeated, also sneering. 'What about you? You haven't any rich relatives, I suppose?'

'Me? Ha ha, I haven't got any rich relatives.'

'Haven't you got any rich relatives? Well, I tell you, you *have* rich relatives. Some of the richest people on earth are your relatives. All the rich country-house owners and Mayfair-flat occupiers are your relatives. All the Rolls-Royce-transported and unlimited expense-account possessors are your relatives. Isn't it bloody horrible you have so many rich relatives, while half the population in Africa, which you own, is half-starving? Isn't it bloody horrible that your relatives have so fleeced Jamaica of all it possessed that the people there are half-starving?' I was warming up and enjoying myself. 'You are so well informed you know all about the Egyptian fellah, do you? Do you know anything of the natives in Kenya? in Rhodesia? in Aden? And worst of all, perhaps, in South Africa? Or are you going to tell me South Africa doesn't belong to your rich relatives? It does. If your rich relatives weren't so happy doing business with those filthy rich there, they would have been scared to flog defenceless black women. Don't you know your rich relatives will send you to South Africa in a second if a few white throats are cut by the natives? But it's the fellah you're worried about, is it? He is in his present plight after being ruled by your rich relatives, the Kitcheners and Co. for sixty years. Whatever happens to him now he can't be worse off than when *your* rich relatives were looking after his welfare.'

Half-way through my speech Vincent had started to grin and he was now smiling broadly. Contact had been made.

'Have a brandy,' he said. He went to the bar and came back with two pints as well as the brandy.

'Misjudged you,' he said. 'My mistake.'

'Whatever you do,' I said, looking at the chess board, 'I can mate you with my black queen.'

'What?' he pretended concern. 'Do you mean to tell me my bishops aren't protecting my king?'

'They're too busy finding excuses for your pawns; besides they're so morally bankrupt in their present position, they're useless.'

'What about my towers?'

'I'm attacking on the left; your left tower has moved so much to the right, it can't come into the battle. Your right tower is so smugly content in its square, it's hardly aware you're being threatened.'

'And my knights?'

'And your knights,' I repeated slowly, trying hard to find something to say, 'are . . .' then I noticed they were off the board, 'not in the battle. This being a moral issue and not one of sheer strength.'

'That's where you are wrong,' he said. 'Watch this.' He moved a pawn forward which changed the whole situation and I was now threatened.

'Alas,' I said, 'yes . . . the Steve Wards.' He burst out laughing.

'Have you been talking to that moron?'

'His mother very kindly asked us to tea.'

'Mrs Ward is a sweet old soul,' he said.

'We met her on a bus one day and she asked us to tea. Her Steve had never met the "natives" it seems. Incidentally, did he ever walk in the streets of Suez?'

'Why do you ask?'

I explained about his advice to us and learnt that he had never set his foot outside the camp. Vincent knew through Shirley, his sister.

'He was repeating barracks talk,' he said.

'What makes a man like Steve wear a uniform and point his gun at wogs and such like?' I asked.

'I told you, he's a moron. I suppose you're going to tell me the Egyptian soldier isn't a moron too?'

'Jesus,' I said, 'the Egyptian soldier hasn't got a nice house with a fireplace and books around it, and a girl friend with high heels, and money to buy beer with, and "civilization" to sacrifice for an army life.'

'That's exactly what Steve is being told he is fighting for. He believes his home is being threatened.'

'Oh, come on, Vincent. You know very well he doesn't know what he's fighting for; he just feels proud wearing an army uniform and fighting for the queen and showing the "savages" how mighty he is.'

'I suppose Steve Ward is the only one knows why Steve Ward is fighting.'

'Let's ask him,' I suggested.

I looked at them at the other table. Font and Edna were wearing the expression of duty being carried out. Every now and then they looked at Mrs Ward and smiled. Steve, always polite and attentive, was passing his cigarettes around. Edna and Shirley said a few words to each other

now and then. Mrs Ward seemed to be the only one enjoying herself with her glass of Guinness in front of her and
her son and future daughter-in-law looking after her.

'Steve and I were at school together,' Vincent said. 'He
knows I consider him a moron and he considers me yellow
and a traitor. I did all I could to get out of the army. I pretended I was half deaf.'

'Why?'

'Sorry to disappoint you. I was following a correspondence
course for television engineering and had a good job in sight.
If the army had paid me fifteen pounds a week I would have
worn any uniform they wished and pointed my gun in any
direction they asked me to.'

If we now went and asked Steve why he fought, I was
thinking, an entirely new world of characters and voices
and tempers and words would be created right there in the
pub. I felt a desire to participate and to watch. But the sight
of Mrs Ward sitting happily drinking her beer decided me
not to spoil her evening. Vincent agreed, but told me she
usually left for home much earlier than the rest. I said we
should go and sit with them. Vincent hesitated for a while.
Shirley had made him promise not to annoy Steve. But after
a while we abandoned the chess game and he came with me.

I apologized for having left them, explaining that my
passion for chess was so consuming, the sight of a chess-
board all but drove me frantic. I was sarcastic. I couldn't
understand what was happening to me. I knew I wanted to
lose my temper and expose something or other, but what
exactly, I didn't know. Perhaps I was unconsciously admit-
ting and being disgusted by an element of insincerity in the
occasion: after all, what made Edna and Font and me go to

Mrs Ward's and accept her hospitality, and be bored, if there wasn't something self-reflecting in our behaviour? Worst of all, perhaps, was the knowledge that when we left them and went home, we would say how 'nice' it was to have been to Mrs Ward's. Mrs Ward *was* nice of course, but the three of us were being bored. Why, then pretend it was being enjoyable? Or even interesting? It was not only that we were pretending to each other, we were also trying to fool ourselves. I say this now, but at the time I had no idea why I felt unsatisfied and ready to provoke unconventional behaviour in myself and everyone else.

Mrs Ward left after a while. We thanked her again for having asked us to tea, and Font insisted on seeing her home. Edna was being cold towards me, but I had reached that stage of insobriety which magnifies self-confidence to a degree of smugness. I turned to Shirley and, without in the least meaning to, I whispered that she was the most attractive girl I had seen for a long time, then immediately I ignored her again. This, I thought, was the most skilful opening; awakening a woman's interest and then ignoring her, and letting her pursue for a while, if only out of sheer curiosity. How it came about that I, certainly inexperienced in the complicated relationship between man and woman should have evolved such theories on courtship, I don't know. There must be a certain instinct in man, more developed in some than in others, which prompts him to act in the most suitable way.

Font returned and I started talking to him. Edna and Vincent seemed to have taken to each other and were carried away by their conversation. Steve must have had a weak bladder because he kept popping downstairs.

'Hello, Fonty Wonty,' I said. 'Here we are, drinking pints of beer in the land of Billy Bunter, and Vincent is William Brown grown up and the landlord is Winnie the Pooh turned publican and on this very table Sir Roger de Coverley wrote his elegant stupidities. Aren't you happy?'

'What's happening to you, Ram?' he said. 'You're changing so fast I'm beginning not to recognize you.'

'I'm only having a good time, Font. Excuse me while I proceed to do so.' I turned to Shirley whose gloves had fallen down, picked them up, and told her there was a very precious flower in Egypt, of which the smell of her hair reminded me.

'You're very naughty,' she said.

'Naughty?' I pretended to be angry. 'You are a very beautiful woman,' I said, 'and you know it. I realize you are engaged to someone else, but you must remember I am not a sophisticated European and so cannot hide my emotions. Since you are beautiful, it is natural for me to admire you and to be incapable of pretending you are just any woman.'

'I am sorry,' she said, 'I did not mean to hurt your feelings.' I turned to Font, acting hurt.

'Jesus, Font; I'm enjoying myself.' I took all the empty glasses and came back with a round of drinks. We were all drinking beer, but I brought Shirley a sherry instead.

'How did you know I like sherry?' she asked. I didn't answer and turned to Font.

'What's the matter with you, Font?' I asked. 'You are the one who's acting strange. Why aren't you enjoying yourself? Why aren't you full to the brim with your own

93

silent ecstasy? Why aren't you in love? Why aren't you overflowing with happiness?'

'Don't force yourself too much, Ram.'

'Jesus, Font. Do you remember that day before the summer holidays at the university, and telling me what a horrid thing it was to go to Alexandria and do over and over again what we had been doing for years and years? And yet, here we are in London, but you are silent and miserable.'

'I am not miserable,' he said. 'I am enjoying myself in my own way; although I never knew up to now how different my way is from yours.'

I drank my beer. Was I enjoying myself? The questions I was beginning to ask myself would kill me, I thought. Why couldn't I do what I was doing without all this judging? Why couldn't I just be what I was only a few weeks earlier in Egypt?

'Are you angry?' Shirley asked me.

I looked at her and suddenly caught her hand under the table and held it tight in mine. Of course I was enjoying myself. Steve went downstairs for about the twentieth time. He didn't look very happy, although of course he didn't know what was going on between Shirley and me.

'Well,' Vincent said, 'shall we ask him?'

'If you wish,' I said.

'What is it?' Shirley asked me. I squeezed her hand and told her we were going to ask Steve how many wogs he had killed.

'Vincent,' she shouted, 'leave Steve alone.' He laughed.

'Edna,' she said, 'please ask Vincent not to be horrible to Steve.'

94

'Of course he won't,' Edna said. 'And anyway I am sure Steve can look after himself.'

'But he can't,' Shirley said. 'He gets all worked up and he'll spend days on end telling me my brother is not fit to be an Englishman.' We all laughed.

Steve came back and pulled a chair near Shirley, who quickly took her hand away from mine. I watched him clumsily putting his arm round Shirley, and the matter-of-fact way she allowed him to do so. I felt sure she didn't love him.

'What was the beer like, in Suez?' I asked Steve. After all we had been to his house, and it would be unfair to gang up against him. As it was, however, he was more or less responsible for what happened.

'We drank the beer the wogs drank there; all right once you get used to it.'

'How did you like the wogs, Stevey boy?' Vincent asked.

'Shut up, Vince,' Shirley said; and she turned to Steve. 'Can't you see you're being rude, using that word?'

'Oo's being rude?' he asked, genuinely puzzled.

'I don't think Edna, Font and Ram like being called wogs at all,' Shirley told him.

'Blimey,' he shouted, 'I haven't called them anything of the sort.'

'No, of course you haven't,' Edna said quickly, 'Shirley is only pulling your leg. Come on; let's drink this one up and let me buy the next round.'

'Your leg's not being pulled,' Vincent said, 'but you keep putting your foot in it.'

'What the hell are you talking about?' Steve shouted. 'What has a filthy wog got to do with these people here?'

'You've put your *other* foot in it now,' Vincent screamed.

'Steve,' Shirley said, 'I know you're a fathead, but I didn't know you were *that* big a fathead. When you say "wogs" you mean Egyptians in general. Edna, Font and Ram are Egyptians.'

The truth suddenly dawned upon him. I felt sorry for him.

'Blimey,' he said, 'I didn't mean to be offensive at all . . . I . . .' The three of us outdid each other in reassuring him.

'What I say is,' he said, 'we're all human beings.'

'That's right,' we said.

'There is no difference between one man and another,' he said.

'All except between you and me,' Vincent said, but we decided to ignore Vincent.

'Mind you,' Steve said, 'I can tell you who's brewing up all the trouble there.'

'Do tell us,' Vincent said.

'It's them ruddy Jews,' he said.

Vincent's laughter echoed all over the pub. 'You've put your very *head* in it this time,' he managed to ejaculate in between fits of guffaws.

Font whispered we should explain Edna was not my sister, since Vincent already knew.

'Edna is Jewish,' I told Shirley.

'Edna is Jewish,' Shirley told Steve.

'How are the Jews causing all the trouble there?' Edna asked Steve.

'Look, I didn't know you were a Jewess,' he said. 'Don't forget we fought the last war for you.'

It was my turn to laugh.

'No, no,' Font said in his intense way. 'The Jews were being persecuted long before you declared war.' He went on to talk about Munich and all that.

'Oh shut up, Font,' I said.

'Why should he shut up?' Edna asked quietly.

'Do you think Steve is going to be convinced of what is true and what is not?' I asked her. 'Don't you know the history of the First World War and how Lenin published the secret reasons for the war and yet millions of Steves went on slaughtering each other for "Honour" and for decorations and didn't care two hoots whether it was for the oil they were doing it? Haven't you read Sassoon and Robert Graves?'

'Let's talk of something else,' Shirley said.

'Be quiet, Shirley,' Vincent told her. Then he turned to Edna and said: 'I've fed that girl books the way a mother does her child milk. Spoons and *shovels* full of books. And then she takes up with this moron because "he's steady and hard-working",' he mimicked. 'Makes me want to spit.'

'I'm a darned sight better than you,' Steve shouted and stood up threateningly. I stood up too, and told Steve to sit down and let's have a drink and not quarrel.

'Go to hell you . . . wog,' he said. I sat down and Shirley jumped up.

'If you don't apologize this very instant, I'll have nothing more to do with you,' she shouted.

'That's right,' he screamed, 'you take sides with these wogs and Jews and that yellow brother of yours.'

I went down to the toilet, and after relieving myself I just idled for a while, looking at myself in the mirror and thinking of nothing in particular.

Steve had gone when I returned. As soon as I sat down Shirley's hand slid into mine.

'Let's go and call Steve back,' I said.

'No,' Shirley said, caressing my hand.

Our hands were under the table and I was hoping no one was noticing what was going on. I wondered what Edna would do if she discovered this; and then wondered what I would do if I discovered Edna and Vincent were holding hands. Nothing, I thought. I was lost in these possibilities when I noticed we were all nearly drunk. We were sitting bleary eyed in silence.

'Let's go and dance,' I suggested. 'Let's drink some more and have more fights and reach a real climax as the Hemingway people in Spain do. Come on, Edna, let's *live*.'

'All right,' she said and pulled us all up. We lost our stupor. Vincent owned an old Austin car, and went to fetch it.

'Ring up Brenda Dungate,' I told Font. 'She might come with us.'

He brightened at the prospect and we looked for her number together. I heard him speak to Dr Dungate first and ask him whether he might take Brenda out dancing. Brenda came to the telephone and Font said we'd pick her up in twenty minutes.

'Font,' I said, 'let's nip to the public bar and have a quick one together.'

As we stood at the bar drinking half pints, I realized for the first time how very fond of Font I was. It struck me that we had always been together since childhood and that we were closer to each other than to anyone else. There was no reason to think of it just then except, perhaps, that I felt I was drifting away from him. But why was I drifting away? I knew something was happening to me, but what, I couldn't tell.

'What's the matter with me, Font?'

'You're becoming phoney, Ram.'

'But that's what I don't know. When I left you all and played chess with Vincent, I was thinking you and Edna were being phoney because you were pretending to be enjoying yourselves, and that I was not being phoney because I preferred to play chess and did so. Then I drank a bit and delivered a tirade against the English to Vincent; but it was all pretence because I was enjoying myself. Then I started making love to Shirley for no reason at all, except, perhaps, for ego's sake. Jesus, I'm even using a word like "ego". And then I enjoyed seeing us making a fool of Steve, although in actual fact I was sorry for him and bore him no grudge whatsoever.'

'You're becoming self-centred, Ram.'

'We never talked of "self-centredness" or "phoniness" when we were in Egypt. These words are beginning to play a part in our life which they never did hitherto.' And then I split into two again, and one part watched me speak to Font, and heard me say 'hitherto'. Why that word 'hitherto' caused the split I don't know. I had forgotten my fear of drifting away from Font. I hardly listened to him as he spoke.

We picked up Brenda and went to a dance. I think it was in Hampstead Town Hall. There were chairs all round the hall, and somehow we all lost each other; Vincent with Edna, Font with Brenda and Shirley with me. To start with I enjoyed the actual dancing, but after a while it was only a matter of holding a new body close to mine and kissing its ears and hearing it pant. We drank some more and acted like lovers. There was not going to be any 'Hemingway' climax after all. I felt like going to bed. I found Edna and told her I was taking Shirley home, then going to bed.

We had a coffee first in an espresso bar. Shirley sat under a red light. She looked very young and wholesome under that colour. We spoke in subdued, friendly voices and talked about each other. The lust of the dance hall had evaporated and left a residue of friendliness and ease in each other's company. She asked me about Edna and I told her she was a very good friend to Font and me. She spoke to me about her life at home and about Steve and about Vincent. Her father had been a drunkard. Her mother had taken the two children away, only to fall in love with Paddy, a young Irishman. Paddy was a chronic non-worker, and they had gone through some hard times. Vincent had always been very intelligent and Paddy, who was a bit of a thinker in his way, had encouraged him to study and was hoping to see him through university. However, the war came, and Paddy was thrown in and out of prisons for refusing to join the British Army. Vincent's hope had vanished. But all the same he managed to study television engineering at night school and had landed a good job. Vincent had tried hard to elevate his sister to his own standard of education; but somehow she was content to become a typist. They had known Steve since childhood. He was an honest, straightforward person and, because her home was sometimes unpleasant with fights between Vincent and Paddy, she had let herself drift into getting engaged to Steve.

I was content, sitting there listening to her. What was it,

I wondered, that I liked about Vincent and Shirley? With them I forgot I was Egyptian and they English and I a stranger in their midst. No matter how hard the Dungates tried, they were never to make me feel we were one and the same. Sitting with Shirley that evening, I returned to my old self and was nothing else but Ram who was born in Cairo and who liked to read and to drink. I felt at ease – Shirley and Vincent were a bit of Font to me. She asked me if I were in love with Edna.

'Yes,' I said.

We walked, hand in hand, to where she lived in St John's Wood. We talked easily and I told her I was sorry about what happened to Steve and confessed I was indirectly responsible. We came to some street-lamps lying on the pavement, waiting to be erected, and Shirley walked along one of them, balancing herself and catching my hand now and then for support.

'I love my brother very much,' she said, 'and I know what he says about Steve is true. He will be a good husband but it will be boring living with him. Vince tells me he'll always remind me I'm being bored.' She jumped off the lamp-post and said: 'I know you were just flirting with me in the pub, but I was excited all the same, and I never once felt excited with Steve.'

We turned into her street. In front of her house a shadow suddenly appeared from the darkness and before I could notice anything else, I received a blow on the nose and was blinded by the tears which usually flow when the nose has been hit.

'I'll murder you, you dirty wog,' he screamed. It was Steve. My nose was bleeding and I bent my head backwards to try and stop the flow. Even at that moment I realized he was very drunk and I didn't feel any anger.

'Steve, if you don't go away this very instant, I'll scream for Paddy.'

'I'll do that Irishman too,' he screamed.

If only I could be angry, I told myself, I could knock that Steve out. But I can never hit someone unless I am angry.

'You know why you are despicable?' I told him. 'It's because you can fight and kill people without being angry. I'm unable to hit you back simply because I feel no anger towards you.'

A door opened and a huge man came out. He wore trousers and singlet and was barefoot.

'Paddy,' Shirley ran to him, 'tell Steve to go home, he's drunk.'

'You bloody Irishman,' Steve shouted.

Shirley pulled me inside and closed the door. We were standing in a kitchen; the gas oven was burning low with its door open, and on the floor was a mattress on which Paddy had probably been sleeping. We heard shouts outside, then Paddy came in.

'Be Jeez,' he said, 'be sure now and don't go out again; I'm tellin' yer that Steve's in a terrible state now.' It was the first time I had heard an Irish brogue. Paddy was a handsome man with a full crop of white hair.

'Ram is Egyptian,' Shirley said.

'Be Jeez,' he said, 'your nose is bleedin' now. I'm tellin' yer now, don't let none of these English touch yer; they've taken enough out of your cahntry as it is. I've seen things when I was a child now, you will not believe when I tell yer. I remember once in Cork . . .'

'You tell him about it some other time,' Shirley said. 'Come in the front room,' she told me.

I said good night and followed Shirley into the front room. My nose had stopped bleeding. The loss of blood had cleared my head and made me feel light and cheerful.

'That was Paddy,' Shirley said, 'what do you think of him?'

'Be Jeez,' I said, 'I loike him.'

'We have terrible fights; but lazy good-for-nothing swine as he is, Vincent and I love him. I'll get some blankets,' she said. We were whispering although there was no reason for it. It's strange how people instinctively whisper when it's dark. We hadn't put the lights on.

'I'll go back to the hotel,' I said.

'The buses have stopped. But you can wait for Vince if you wish and he'll drive you home.' As she said this we heard his car outside, then his voice talking to Paddy. He knocked at the door and came in.

'Hello, Ram,' he said, half laughing, 'you've tasted an English fist I hear. How are you?'

'I'm all right,' I said, also laughing.

'You mustn't hate Steve too much, you know. He's really a very decent boy.'

'Jesus, I don't hate him at all,' I said. 'If anything I'm ashamed of myself for what happened.

'Let's forget Steve, now,' Shirley said. 'Vince, can you drive Ram home?'

'Yes,' he said, 'but why don't you sleep here? I've got some beer and we can talk for a while.'

'All right,' I said.

He put the lights on, then switched them off again. They were stark lights and the room was cosier with just the light

103

which came in from a street-lamp. He fetched glasses and beer.

'Let's ask Paddy to drink, too,' I said.

'Oh dear,' Shirley said. 'All right.'

I was sitting on the sofa and Paddy on an armchair opposite. Vincent and Shirley were on the floor, Shirley resting her back against my legs. We talked until four in the morning. We just talked, and drank beer, and smoked. I told them the fellah lived exactly the same way he did ten thousand years ago . . . even to the houses he built and the way he whirled the water from the Nile to his land. At last we were all sleepy. Paddy and Vincent went to bed while Shirley went for some blankets. I kissed her affectionately and as soon as she left I took my clothes off and lay down.

It had been a pleasant time, yet there was something lacking . . . a sense of climax. There is only one perfect ending to everything, and that is death, but there are other good endings as well. In spite of all that happened that day, and the nice *conclusion* of talking quietly in the darkness, there was a vestige of frustration in me as I lay there. And then I heard the door open and felt her warm body next to mine. This was the good ending. Even though we did not love each other, even if there was no lust between us, just to caress and kiss and to sleep close to one another was the final touch to end the day. And I understood how some men have to reach that fulfilment even between man and man.

I was wrong to think caressing Shirley's body was the climax to that day. There was another end to it when I returned to the hotel.

I slipped away from Shirley's house quietly, early in the

morning, without waking anyone. I went to Edna's room as soon as I reached the hotel.

'I've been unfaithful to you,' I said.

'I know,' she said.

'Aren't you jealous?'

'Do you want me to be?'

'I want you to be passionately jealous and threaten suicide and weep and lament and . . . isn't there another word similar to weep and lament? . . . and strew ashes over yourself. Edna, what was the idea behind these Biblical people who strewed ashes over themselves when they were unhappy?'

'I don't know,' she said.

'Edna, what is this? What is happening to me? I am Egyptian and have lived in Egypt all my life and suddenly I am here, and at the end of three weeks I have slid into this strange life where I meet a girl and think it natural to go to bed with her at the end of the day, under the same roof as her brother and mother and Paddy, and find it natural they find it natural that she sleeps with me if she wants to. Such things don't happen in Egypt, so how can I come here and live in an entirely different manner and yet feel I have been living like this all my life? What will happen to me when I go back to Egypt? Have you ever met my friends Yehia and Jameel and Fawzi? I'm not going to apologize for having spent the night with Shirley. You don't love me and I don't in the least feel guilty about it. I haven't slept much and am rather tired; perhaps that's why I want to speak the truth. Look, Edna; don't attribute to me qualities I don't possess. I just like to gamble and drink and make love and no matter what act I put on, you should know the truth.'

'I've told you before, Egyptians are not found in Cairo or in Alexandria,' she said. 'You've never really known Egyptians. I hate Egyptians of your class as much as I do my parents.'

'What am I, then, if I am not Egyptian?'

'You are what you are; and that is a human being who was born in Egypt, who went to an English public school, who has read a lot of books, and who has an imagination. But to say that you are this or that or Egyptian, is nonsense.'

'What are you, Edna?'

'I can't be generalized about either, except that I was born Jewish. But the difference between you and me is that I *know* Egyptians and love them.'

'Edna,' I said, 'you said I was well read and had an imagination. I'm also intelligent. Intelligent enough to know you are not in love with me . . .'

'That's the second time you've said I don't love you.'

'. . . and to wonder,' I went on, 'why you befriended Font and me and why you are being so generous to both of us. Let me be frank. Font is a lovable person and I can understand you may have genuine affection for him. But as for myself, since I set foot in London, my character has changed, or perhaps my real character has suddenly emerged. I am neither "lovable" nor "sweet" nor "nice"; on the contrary, I'm a conceited, arrogant, all-knowing, unlikeable creature. So I wonder why you don't tell me that to my face. Perhaps you feel responsible because you brought me here. But here and now I absolve you of all responsibility. Edna, please, let us shed all vestige of sophistication and "double-talk" this instant and let us tell each other the truth. Tell me about yourself, Edna.'

She closed her eyes and lay still for a moment. I took my shoes off and curled into an armchair.

'My family has been in Egypt for more than five generations,' she started. 'I am the first person in the family to speak Arabic. I had a Greek nurse called Rosa who was married to an Egyptian policeman. My parents used to go on long trips and leave me in Rosa's care. She used to take me secretly to live with her husband and his family in a small village. At first I was disgusted with the dirt and the lack of comfort; the cows and chicken as much inmates of the house as we. But I went more often to the village and loved every person in it. They would never accept a gift without returning it ten times over, no matter how poor they were. I loved the way they woke up at dawn and worked till sunset then lay to sleep either in their mud-huts or in the field. I loved the dignity the fellah possesses and which no one who hasn't lived with him knows anything about. I loved the way they helped each other naturally and all took responsibility for the many orphans there. At home my parents and their Egyptian friends used to say "he is nothing but a fellah" about someone they considered ill-mannered and vulgar. I was very lonely as I grew up. I found nothing attractive about my friends, whether they were Jews, Europeans, or Egyptians.

'Rosa's husband had a young brother of my age. His name was Adle. He had very large brown eyes with long eye-lashes. He would never have anything to do with me. He never accepted a gift from me and never spoke to me. His brother bought him a pair of trousers and a shirt once, but he never wore them in my presence. He insisted on remaining barefoot whenever I was there. I used to watch him from my window each morning, washing under the village pump. I was very much in love with him. From the age of fourteen I loved him with every fibre in my body.

'When I was eighteen, we were living in Alexandria. Rosa's husband had also been transferred to Alexandria and managed to bring Adle with him and to put him in the police force. Rose told me Adle never accepted a bribe in his life, although all the other policemen did – they had to. I gave myself to Adle that summer. I wanted to marry him and give him everything he lacked in his life. But he refused. Rosa gave me hope; she told me he whispered my name in his sleep.'

She was speaking her sentences slowly and one at a time, with pauses in between.

'Suddenly I was taken to Europe by my parents. I was supposed to return in two months, but they enrolled me in a university and returned without me. I wrote hundreds of letters to Adle in Arabic, but he never answered. I realized the only thing I could do was to try and forget him.' She paused.

'I returned at the end of two years. A few months after the end of the war between Israel and Egypt in 'forty-eight.' She paused again and took a deep breath.

'With the help of their Egyptian friends, my parents had bribed the necessary people and brought an action against Adle for ''inciting'' me. He refused to utter one word in his defence. He was put in prison for four months. All this took place while I was in Europe. I had no idea my father knew anything about Adle. Rosa, of course, was not with us any more when I returned to Egypt. It was she who told me all about it, when I finally found her. She also told me Adle had died in the war between Israel and Egypt.'

'Enough,' I wanted to tell her. 'Enough. I don't want to hear about such things. I'll take an academic interest in politics and injustice, if you wish, but keep these real things away from me. I don't mind *reading* about them, but keep your story away from me.'

'What did you do, Edna,' I whispered.

'I joined the Communist Party. I worked like a slave for it. I wanted to kill my own personal life and only be an organ of the Party. The Party has always had to be clandestine in Egypt. I met the cream of humanity in it; Egyptians, Jews, Greeks. Inevitably, we were discovered. My father once again used his money and I was rushed to England. Then the revolution in Egypt took place and I rushed back to fight for it and with it and support it. But who could use me? I am a Jewess.'

I didn't move or say anything for a long time.

'Are you asleep, Edna?'

'No, Ram.'

I was miserable. I remembered my cheap facetiousness – 'weep' and 'lament' and I wanted to bleed to death at her feet in repentance. I learnt at that moment that when a situation is very real and true, all this business of splitting into two and watching oneself act, is far away and dead and non-existent.

'I first saw you and Font about twelve years ago,' she said, 'you were about eleven then. It was your cousin Mounir's birthday. I was with the grown-ups and saw you and Font leave all the other children and play with the gardener's son and give him the enormous amount of cakes and crackers you were hoarding in your pockets. I had been wondering why you kept filling your pockets with everything on the table. I always remembered that scene whenever I went to the village with Rosa. Then I saw you again at your aunt's that day you made a mess of her party. Do you understand, now, it was natural for me not to want to lose you and Font? I was very happy that year we spent in Cairo together. You were so honest and sincere, both of you.'

Another period of silence.

'I, too, was very happy that year before we came here,' I said. 'It is natural for me to be wholly and completely in love with you. You are, to me, an unearthly creature which, for some reason or another, bestows some of its exquisiteness upon me. I have so much respect for you, and I am so awed by the fact that you allow me to love you . . .'

'Ram,' she said.

'Yes?'

She didn't answer.

'What is it, Edna?'

'I am not as good as you think I am.'

I smiled.

That was the only time Edna used the cliché language of lovers, and I ignored it.

'Tell me what you are thinking,' she said after a while.

'You know how much I have always read? Well, some-how, although I read and read, it was only reading. I mean I never thought what I read had anything to do with life. No, what I mean is, I never imagined that I could be "a character" . . . I'm not explaining myself properly. What I mean is, what I read were just stories, and . . .'

'I understand what you mean, Ram.'

'Well, and then somehow, when I came here, or perhaps just before I came here, I unconsciously realized that I, also, could "live". Perhaps what I am saying is not true. I mean, perhaps there is no reason or excuse for the way I am beginning to behave; perhaps it's just my character and that's all there is to it. But I've said that already.'

'No, it isn't your character,' she said.

'Anyway, Edna; I have decided to . . .' I had decided nothing at all, it just came to me as I spoke to her, '. . . leave the hotel today.'

'Where to?'

'I don't know yet. But I am going to try and find a cheap room somewhere or other, perhaps in the East End, and I am going to follow that course at the polytechnic, whatever it is. I think it is mathematics or chemistry or something like that. That is the best thing for me to do now, to – excuse the expression – "find myself".'

'Ram, dear, are you sure a room in the East End is not a part of the books you have read?'

'Perhaps,' I replied.

She smiled, but there was no sarcasm in her smile.

'Come here,' she said.

I went and sat facing her on the edge of the bed. She pulled me towards her and held me tight against her breast.

'I do love you, Ram,' she said.

'I love you too,' I said, 'very much.'

She took her arms away from me and asked me if I had enough money.

'Yes,' I said.

I was glad to find that Font was not in our rooms. I packed my things and left them with the hotel porter. Edna was paying the hotel. Of the fifty pounds I had when I arrived in London, eleven were left.

'Are you coloured?' she asked. I looked at my hands to see whether I was coloured. Although I had read so much about this in Egypt, I had never encountered it in actual life. I had never wondered whether I was coloured or not (later I went to a library and learnt that I was white).

'I don't know,' I said.

She was a fat woman with a mop in her hand.

'It's nothing to do with me, dear. They've told me if you were coloured I was to say the room was already let. You look white enough to me, but you never know.'

'I am Egyptian,' I said.

She told me to wait for a moment and closed the door.

'Egyptian, ma'am, is that all right?' I heard her shout.

She opened the door a moment later and told me to come in. This was in South Kensington. I had obtained the address from a notice board outside the Underground station.

A thin-lipped, long-nosed woman said 'how-d'you-do' through her nose and asked me to sit down.

'You are a student, I suppose,' she said. 'My husband, Captain Treford, and I were in Egypt, you know. We met a surprising number of very intelligent Egyptians there at the Gezira Sporting Club.'

I was well-dressed, with a snow-white handkerchief sticking out of my breast pocket, and a pair of light brown leather gloves in my hand.

'I wonder if you know the Kamals,' she said, 'Mrs Kamal – Sophie – was a very dear friend of mine.'

'I know her,' I said. 'She's my cousin.'

'How lovely!' Captain Treford's wife clapped her hands. 'Sophie is such a *wonderful* person.'

'She's a pig,' I said.

'I beg your pardon?'

'I said my cousin Sophie is nothing but a pig.'

'Really?' she drawled. 'Perhaps we are not talking of the same person.'

'Do you know Dr Khairy and his wife?' I asked.

'Why yes, we often played bridge with them and went to their charming villa in . . .'

'Well, they're also pigs,' I said.

'You must understand, Mr . . . Mr . . .'

'Font,' I said.

'You must understand, Mr Font, that the Captain and myself have decided to let the room purely out of a sense of social duty . . .'

'Excellent,' I interrupted in a rich and easy manner, 'you should give it free of rent.'

'Ooha ooha ooha,' she laughed through her nostrils; 'we can hardly do *that* . . . ooha ooha. And so, Mr Flint,' she continued from where I had interrupted, 'you will have to keep your little jokes to yourself.'

'Yes indeed, Mrs Trickleford,' I said, and uttered three oohas. 'Do you think ten guineas . . . a week of course . . . would be suitable?'

She jumped up and said certainly, certainly, and anyhow it wasn't a matter of money at all. In fact she was very pleased to do Sophie a good turn, even though, between her and me, Sophie could be a bit of a . . . of a . . .

'Pig,' I said. 'I won't bother to see the room now, but I

shall send my chauffeur over with my bags. You don't happen to have a garage? . . . It's a Bentley,' I added.

I left, but somehow didn't feel as victorious as I might have been. After walking in the East End for a whole day, I decided I wouldn't like to live there after all. On the third day I took a room in Battersea with a mechanic's family: a small room with a hospital bed, a sink, a table and chair and nothing else. But I had an independent entrance and it was cheap and, anyhow, it had 'colour', and, strangely enough, I began to 'live'. Of course no one who 'lives' in the sense I mean knows he is living; it is only when he ceases to 'live' that he realizes it.

I hadn't seen or telephoned Font or Edna until I found that room in Battersea. Then I went to see them. I had five pounds left.

I found Font packing. He was disgusted with me, he said. I could at least have told him I was leaving the hotel, and as for flirting with Steve's girl friend and sleeping out that night, it was filthy. To think we had gone to Steve's house and accepted his hospitality, and then I'd tried to take his girl away; it made Font want to vomit. I was no better than all these *fils-à-papa* Egyptians who had nothing else to do but to run after every skirt and no scruples about whose skirt it was either. Font had never expressed an opinion about rich Egyptians before. I told him Steve had probably murdered hundreds and hundreds of women and children . . . poor, miserable, innocent children in Aden and all over Africa and Cyprus, and if he thought I was going to have any scruples about Steve, he was wrong. He didn't quite believe me, but put it at the back of his mind for consideration some other time.

'Is Edna in her room?'

'Edna left England yesterday.'

One only realizes the extent of his love when he thinks he has lost the one he loves; and unhappily, very often only begins to love when he feels his love is not returned.

'Don't worry,' Font said, 'she's coming back.'

'Why did she leave, Font?'

'I don't know.'

'Was she angry?'

'No. But she said not to forget we are Egyptian and must return.'

'Jesus, I love her,' I said.

He gave me a typical Font look and told me I possessed a very unorthodox way of showing my love.

'Don't be stupid, Font. What I did with Shirley had nothing to do with being in love with Edna.'

'Forgive me,' he said. 'I haven't quite reached your standard of sophistication.'

'Oh, shut up, Font.'

After a while he showed me two letters. One was from the Home Office.

Dear Sir,

The Under Secretary of State directs me to inform you that your application for an extension of stay in the United Kingdom may not be considered unless proof of adequate means of support is forwarded to him within a week.

Your obedient servant . . .

(I have a number of letters from this obedient servant, the last of which is an answer to a private letter I sent him, telling him he was not an obedient servant at all.)

The other letter was from Didi Nackla in Paris saying she intended coming next summer and would we find her a reasonably priced flat. 'A reasonably priced flat'. Didi Nackla could have bought a castle for the summer if she had wanted to.

'How much money have you got, Font?'

'Fifteen pounds.'

'Between us we have eighteen pounds. The Under Secretary won't consider that adequate for anything.'

'Edna has left us two tickets for Egypt.'

'I am not going to use mine,' I said.

'Neither am I,' he said.

I lay down on the bed while he continued packing. His eyebrows went up and up, then down. Then up again.

'Where are you going, Font?'

'I have to look for a room.' But his eyebrows still ascended and descended.

'What is it, Font?'

'Look, Ram. Edna has left three hundred pounds with me in case we needed them. She has spent enough money on us as it is. I am not going to touch any of that money. But you do what you want.'

'What I want is to touch every bit of this money,' I told him. 'Money? What's money to Edna? She's got tons and tons of it. Why shouldn't we touch it?'

'Do what you want,' he said, and turned his back to me pretending he was very busy packing.

'What's the matter with you, Font?'

'The matter with *me*?'

'I mean what's the matter with you, thinking I am serious

when I say I want that money. Of course I am not going to touch it either.'

'Look, Ram. You've changed since we've come here. I don't know you any more.'

'All right,' I sighed. 'Anyway, I've got a good plan. We can use that money indirectly.'

'What do you mean, indirectly?'

'Just listen to me. We'll put the money in a bank in my name . . .'

'Do as you want,' he said.

'*Shut up*,' I screamed. 'We put that money in the bank in my name, and if you say anything now, I'll murder you; then I ask the bank to give me a note saying that I have three hundred pounds in the bank. I withdraw the money, place it in another bank in *your* name this time, and also obtain a note saying you have deposited that much money. So we've both got ''adequate means of support'' for that Under Secretary's information.'

This idea pleased Font, although he tried not to show it. So I told him to apologize and admit I was the most intelligent, honest, sincere, lovable, and faithful person he had ever known. He had finally closed his suitcase after jumping on it and pushing the lid down for ten minutes. As he refused to repeat what I had said, I opened the suitcase and the lid flew up. We had a friendly tussle and were friends again.

'Let's gamble,' I suggested.

'Who, you and me?'

'Don't be stupid. Let's play poker or something like that with rich people.' But of course we knew no rich people we could play with; so I suggested we go to the race track. But first we had to find a room for Font. I was in high spirits that day. Perhaps it was because Edna had left. After the initial shock of learning she had gone away, I experienced a surge of freedom and, anyway, she was coming back.

We took Font's suitcase downstairs and then went to the nearest pub in which to consider the best way of finding him a room.

But although she sent us money, Edna did not write or return for a year. And when she did come back we became lovers again although she would not marry me and would not give me a reason . . . and my character had really changed. Then Didi Nackla turned up in London and stayed with us for eight months. It's strange that in spite of what happened between Didi Nackla and myself at that time, when I think of London I never think of Didi Nackla.

PART III

Se sacrifier à ses passions, passe;
Mais à des passions qu' on a pas?

GIRODET

I opened my eyes in the morning to the call to the faithful: a beautiful call, mingled with the rustle of a palm tree outside and the noise of Kharafallah putting tables out on the pavement downstairs. Even the shadows on the closed shutter seemed to play in harmony with the call. A beautiful call from a high steeple telling us all about 'No God but God' and who his prophet is. Does it matter who his prophet is? 'No God but a God' would be better, I thought, or just 'No God, no God', but in the same beautiful voice. And who is going to climb those stairs and give us a call if a revolution – a real one – takes place? No one. A sad thought. Yes, I sighed, a beautiful call which has never been described as anything but a 'wail' in the countries whose culture I've lapped up like a puppy.

I looked at Edna sleeping, her scar more conspicuous in the morning, and her hair a mass of tangles on the pillow. Somerset Maugham once described love as the ability of two persons to use the same tooth-brush. Tooth-brush love? I brought my head a bit closer to Edna's and a ripple of breath, of scent, a fine wire of reminiscence of her, Edna, fell softly upon me. The sense of smell is much more a retainer of things past than is the sense of hearing or of sight. We had very seldom spent the whole night together. There had always been an aloofness on her part which I rarely overcame and I had never been able to take her for granted. We had never embraced just out of habit, and my passion for her had always remained intact.

Our bodies, our beings, seem to be filled with venoms and poisons wriggling inside us like snakes wanting to escape. Serpents of sex and love and emotion and longing and frustration coil and uncoil and show their heads now and then. We drown them in alcohol and passion and subdue them at times at the gambling table or even on the football field, but their turgidity returns again and we are faced once more with their torturing pressures. Now and then, they all seem to escape, giving us a respite which we call happiness or contentment or even serenity. I felt light and peaceful as though all my serpents had shrivelled or shrunk or completely escaped for a while. Even my flesh seemed to cling tighter and neater around my bones. Like those Indian ascetics who search for the secret of a serpentless life.

And if, at such moments, you let your thoughts wander, they transcend every-day pettiness and smallness and seem to hover high up, gazing at the world detachedly and even benignly. And a perception, an awareness of the complete scene below is registered with a lucidity and a clarity which you sometimes imagine to come very briefly across during certain stages of drunkenness.

This hovering gaze which could have embraced the whole world in its scan, focused only on Edna, and with a terrible intensity I realized the extent of my love for her and also realized that we would have to part. I saw her bullied by nationalities and races and political events and revolutions and dictatorships and particularly by her own vague idealism. I held her tenderly in my arms and also saw my own shallowness and unworthiness in contrast to her deepness and sincerity.

She opened her eyes. We remained close, looking at one another.

No amount of talking or explaining will really bring two lovers or two friends closer than they can be in silence.

'Please, Ram,' she whispered. 'Go away now.'

I dressed quietly and went out. Downstairs was Yehia's car, which I had borrowed the night before and in which we had driven to the Pyramids.

I drove the car to Yehia's, then walked home.

'Haven't you spent the night here?' my mother asked.

'No.'

'Where, then?'

'I was with Yehia,' I said.

After a while she asked me what Yehia was now doing.

'He's at the university,' I said.

'Really? Hasn't he finished his studies yet?'

'No.'

'Very strange. How long has he been at the university?'

'Ten years.'

'Of course they're very rich,' she said. 'His mother was with me in school, you know. What *fou-rires* at the *pensionnat*! I remember the *mère-supérieure* insisting on putting us in different dormitories, we were such devils when together. She was very lucky, of course; Yehia's father is a man *très comme-il-faut*. Deauville each year, my dear, and one beautiful mistress after another.' She moved her head from side to side in appreciation.

'I went to tante Noumi yesterday,' I said.

'*Tu as bien fait*, Ram. I am very happy you went to see her. I am always hoping you become good friends with your cousin Mounir. He is becoming very influential. *Il est très élégant, ce garçon;* and then think of the future you may have with your aunt's influence behind you. Can't you see yourself, Ambassador in a European country? You have all the qualities for it; tall, good-looking, languages and then, of course, your English education. *Un vrai gentleman*. People like you are very rare nowadays.' Then she said she hoped I hadn't gone empty-handed to my aunt, and I laughed.

'Your father was very considerate in such matters,' she said, 'although he didn't really belong to our milieu. *Dire à quoi nous sommes arrivés*, Ram. You were too young to remember my father's house; what luxury. The servants, handsome Sudanese with starched robes and red bands round their waists . . . even your aunt Noumi doesn't live in the style we were brought up in.'

We both lit cigarettes.

'And what did you tell your aunt?'

'I asked her to give me a thousand pounds,' I said.

'A thousand pounds? Why do you want so much? You haven't been gambling again?'

'No.'

'What, then?'

'Oh, I don't know. I want to go and live in Europe for a while.'

'Be reasonable, my son. *Au fond* I don't blame you. Where is the cosmopolitan life we led? Of course if you get into the Diplomatic Corps . . .'

I went outside to the balcony for a while, then came back.

'As I was telling Mimi yesterday,' my mother continued, 'the boy has travelled and it is difficult for him to work here the same as everyone else.'

'Do you think I can become Ambassador to London?' I asked.

'Why not? Who is our Ambassador there now?'

'There is none.'

'No?'

'No.'

'Why not? Of course you can't become Ambassador straight away; you're too young for one thing.'

'Pity,' I said. I went to my room and lay down on my bed.

Our servant, Corrollos, told me breakfast was ready. He is a Copt like us, Corrollos, with all the characteristic Coptic traits: the slyness and perpetual intrigue, the sychophancy, even his thin face with the blue veins sticking out at the temples, is us. He is always bending down a little, devouring the floor. He has been with us for twenty-five years.

'How is your wife, Corrollos?'

He bent even further down and said she was very sick, bless me for asking.

'And your children?'

God keep me, he was trying to save enough money to have a doctor look at them.

'I'll get one of my doctor friends to see them,' I said.

Impossible, he said. The likes of him could only afford the very cheapest of doctors.

'You'll not have to pay anything.'

He shook his head and brushed the carpet with his *hand*.

'Are you sick, too?'

The Saviour knew, he was not thinking about himself; he was going to die soon anyway.

We Copts have something about being sick. I sprang out of bed and went to my mother.

'You don't look well,' I told her.

'I knew it,' she said. 'I didn't want to tell you, but I am a very sick person. I have never recovered from my operation.'

I smoked after breakfast and then didn't know what to do with myself. I walked three times round my room, then to the balcony, back to my room, and then to the sitting-room and my mother. A propos of nothing she suddenly said she had sacrificed her life for me.

'I know,' I said.

'You cannot imagine . . .'

'I can, Mummy. I *know* you have sacrificed your life for me.'

'Ever since . . .'

'I know,' I said. 'Ever since you married.'

My mother didn't love her husband, and she believes she married him solely to give me a respectable father. The fact that she conceived me two years after her marriage, she finds irrelevant. I was responsible for the whole thing.

'Thank you, Mummy,' I said.

I took a bath and dressed carefully. There is a tailor in old Cairo who has been cutting suits for our family for years. I go to him, choose a cloth, have it tailored, and somehow the bill is mysteriously paid.

'Where are you going?' my mother asked.

I stood at the door jingling the house-keys in my pocket. I didn't know where I was going.

'To the club,' I decided.

There is something about that club. Just walking along the drive from the gate to the club-house, seeing the perfectly-kept lawns on either side, the specially-designed street-lamps hovering above you, the white stones lining the road, the car-park, and then the croquet lawn – *croquet!* a place where middle-aged people play croquet. Imagine being a *member* of a place where middle-aged people play croquet. This ease; this glide from one place to another; the crispy notes in crocodile wallets; the elegant women floating here and there. Mobile sculptures. And then into the club-house, through it, and out to the swimming-pool where members move as though they were a soft breeze.

The strange thing about this club is that in the early days of the revolution, it was condemned as a symbol of exploitation and was taken over by a committee or something like that. Well, all the members are still members, with a few additional military members. I repeat the word 'members' *à propos* the military newcomers, because they too have acquired this floating, breeze-like, ethereal quality.

I put my hand in my pocket and walked slowly towards the club-house. A beautiful open Mercedes drove past me and someone waved. I waved back. We all know each other. We know each other, all about each other, and how much land and money we possess. We also marry between us. The Moslem members marry Moslem members, and the Copts marry Copts.

'Good morning, Ram.'

'Good morning, sir.' We didn't shake hands. If we had carried sticks or umbrellas for support, we would both have stood at an inclined vertical, and anyone watching from a distance would have seen two tulips swaying slightly into a brief encounter. As it was, however, we had no sticks; so we stood, hand in pocket, smiling at each other.

The trouble with me is that I like that. I *like* to put my hand in my pocket with a bit of cuff showing; a suspicion of waistcoat under my coat, and a strip of handkerchief in my breast pocket. I like it. I am *aware* that I like it.

'How are you?'

'Very well, thank you, sir. How is Lady Tannely?'

'Very happy indeed to be back here. She adores this country and considers it her home.' I had lost my virginity to Lady Tannely, so had many of the young members. She took you home when you were sixteen or so, to teach her Arabic, she'd say; and while you were dying of excitement and love, she would be all vivacious and hysterical with anticipation. Then suddenly, you'd find yourself in bed with her and all at once she'd turn into a cold slab of marble who'd tell you, afterwards, 'now wasn't that nice?' A terrible disillusionment.

I speak English without an accent, and yet, talking to him, slowly and involuntarily, an Oxfordish tinge began to colour my speech; and when I tried to erase that accent, I found it difficult to do so. Strange.

'We spent a charming evening at your aunt's residence,' he said. You notice the word 'residence' of course. There it is; *Residence*.

'Charming,' he said.

My aunt considers it suitable for her son Mounir to have Lady Tannely as 'mistress'. (I put the word 'mistress' in inverted commas because you can't have Lady Tannely as mistress. You just f— her.) Hence the charming evenings at my aunt's Pyramid Road villa. Of course Mounir has never so much as touched Lady Tannely. Dinner parties! Jesus, he *is* stupid, that boy. Lady Tannely picks you if she wants you and that's that. I like her, though.

'Do you vote Labour?' I suddenly asked.

'I beg your pardon?'

'Do you vote Labour?' I repeated.

'My dear chap, I've never been interested in politics.'

'Suez,' I said.

'Oh, *that* was a blunder.'

'Twenty-five thousand Egyptians dead,' I exaggerated.

'So many? Oh, *à la guerre comme à la guerre* . . .' and he laughed. I laughed too, and we parted.

The word 'Egypt' evokes in you, I suppose, a scene of a fellah trudging home in the twilight, a spade over his shoulder, and his son leading a cow behind him. Well, Egypt is a place where middle-aged people play croquet. I don't know why this croquet thing suddenly impressed me. I have passed that lawn thousands of times without ever thinking about it. I turned round and sat on a bench to watch some people play. One of them was the same Mimi my mother had mentioned earlier on. All our young Mimis and Tatas and Sousous grow up and get married and have children, and their children have children, but they still remain young Mimis and Tatas and Sousous. This particular Mimi is a tall one with flat feet and a camelly walk. Any moment now, you'd think, she was going to pitch forward and kiss the ground. She has a bit of an Adam's apple too. Together with the Tatas and the Sousous and my mother, she went to the French *pensionnat*. As a child I used to go and fetch my girl cousins from the same *pensionnat*, with the chauffeurs. It was a very severe place and you had to mention the girl's secret number through a small hole before the door was, reluctantly you'd think, just hardly opened and a pale, black-dressed figure emerged and started putting on make-up before it even reached the car.

'Coucou!' Mimi called to me and waved.

'Coucou!' I called back. I tell you, I have been coucou-ing since I learnt to speak, but here I am, my coucou all self-conscious, and I am aware of sitting there calling 'coucou'. It is because of reading an article the day before in the *New Statesman* about the problems of irrigation in India. How can you read an article in the *New Statesman* about the problems of irrigation in India, and then sit down and shout 'coucou'?

'Coucou,' I repeated.

'He's the nephew of . . .' I heard her translate me to a man with a croquet mallet. I watched him, his mallet almost horizontal because of his belly, finally discovering he had to hang it sideways if it were ever to reach the ball. No, but this complete detachment from the game. Later on Mimi would phone my mother and say: 'I played croquet today . . . what fun.'

Mimi swung her neck in my direction and humptily followed it.

'*Cochon*,' she said, playfully brandishing her mallet at me, 'you are causing your mother endless worry with your political nonsense.'

'You look beautiful in those slacks, Mimi,' I said.

'So you don't call me *Tante* Mimi any more? *Cochon*, if I were a few years younger, I'd have an affair with you. I bought them at Kirka. You should see the beautiful things that are starting to come from Italy, Ram; makes all the stuff we've been wearing up to now seem rags. Come and play with us. Do you know who that is?' she whispered. She told me who he was as he came towards us.

'Ha ha ha ha ha ha,' he said very quietly, putting his hand on my shoulder and shaking me slightly. Then he caught the lobe of my ear and pulled it. 'I am a very great friend of your aunt,' he said, 'ha ha ha ha ha.'

'*C'est un homme charmant*,' Mimi told me.

I went up the steps and into the club-house. This solid spaciousness enveloped me in its ease. I could go straight across the entrance hall to the swimming-pool, in the grand veranda, and on down the steps to the playing fields and the foreign governesses, or I could turn right to the bridge room and the lounges. I stood undecided. From where I was, I could see a game of polo was due to start. It is a point of honour with polo players to keep their backs straight. I watched one examining the knee of a horse. He knelt, one knee to the ground in a worshipping posture, and extended his arms in royal elegance. Talk about the son leading the cow behind his father. Dukes of Edinburgh, all.

I felt like having a cold beer and eating salted peanuts by the pool; then a cigarette and another beer and more peanuts. I could do it, of course, even though I had no money. But I knew the pattern too well; the depression afterwards and the self-disgust.

I watched the swimmers. The club has no uniform, but there is a tiny, never-mentioned badge you wear when you are swimming. It doesn't matter how expensive your bathing costume is, if it doesn't bear the sign of Jantzen – a woman diving – you are not a genuine member. I remember one of my girl-cousins having a costume specially knit for her, and the matter-of-fact way she sewed an old Jantzen badge to it. That's the trouble with me, you see. I stand there being bloody superior, and then I remember that my bathing costume also bears the sign of the *élite*. I remember that I have played croquet, and that if I played polo, I also would keep my back straight. No, I thought, definitely no drinking today.

'Ram Bey. They are looking for a fourth in the bridge

room.' The servants in the club have seen us grow up and call us by our Christian names, adding such honorific titles as 'Bey' and 'Pasha'.

'Who are they, Hassan?'

'Your cousin Mounir,' he said, 'and two American ladies.'

'Which ones, Hassan?'

'They are new, Ram Bey.' Then he told me they were very pretty. I had to be careful, since if I lost, I wouldn't be able to pay.

'Who is behind the bar this morning?'

'Ali.' That was bad. He refuses to lend money out of the till.

'Half-half,' Hassan said in English, and slipped me a five-pound note. 'But please, Ram Bey, do not partner Mounir Effendi.' There you are – Effendi being the least of the honorific titles.

The last time I had seen Mounir had been in a night-club, and then we had just ignored each other. Hassan vanished and I walked slowly towards the bridge room.

'Hi there, Ram, how are things?' my cousin Mounir shouted. 'Sure am glad to see you. We're looking for a fourth; inclined?'

'Inclined,' I said, 'in a horizontal way.' Which was stupid, but there is something about Mounir which drives me to say and do things alien to my nature. His American accent irritated me as usual, although only a short while earlier I myself had put on an accent with Lady Tannely's husband. I pretended I wasn't particularly noticing the two women he was with. They were both pretty in that neat and smart American way; the type you imagine to be of Scandinavian origin; a bit hard. Women, you feel, who can look after themselves and so have sacrificed a bit of their femininity. Intelligent to a certain limit, although they would never recognize that limit. But very attractive.

One of them, slightly older than the other, said: 'I'm Caroline, and that's Sue. Now let's get this straight; do you play Culbertson and the Blackwood-four-no-trumps, or are you Acol?' I didn't like her.

'I'm Ram,' I said, and shook hands with them, which seemed rather a strange thing to do.

'Sure is nice to play with you again, Ram. What . . .'

'Whisky,' I said.

'This guy's my cousin,' he said.

'We'll cut for partners,' I said, ignoring Mounir, 'and not change.'

'Why not?' Caroline asked.

'You get to know your partner's game.'

'Sue and I will play together,' she said.

'We'll cut,' I insisted. There was a war going on between this Caroline and myself already. It seems difficult to imagine that there was an age when man was gallant to woman and kissed her hand and her desire was a command. To me, it is a little bit possible to imagine such a time, because gallantries, in Egypt, are still practised after a fashion and welcomed by the women. But I know that to be conspicuously gallant to the average European or American woman, makes her despise you. I don't know why I think of that, except that this very hostility at the beginning with women I find attractive always seems to lead to something more than a passing acquaintance.

'How much are we playing for?' I asked.

'A pound a hundred,' Caroline said. A pound a hundred. I have played a pound a hundred before, but then it was gambling, real gambling with my sleeves rolled, and drinking coffee, and a dozen people watching. An event, what. The five pounds in my pocket suddenly became worth a shilling.

'Sure thing,' Mounir said, 'it's the usual.' The liar; but then he loves to take his cheque book out and sign a cheque. He looked at me. He knew he'd have to pay my losses if I didn't win.

'All right,' I said.

We decided to cut for partners after all and I found myself stuck with Mounir, when he suddenly shouted: 'For cryin' out loud, this deck's been used before!' This is typical Mounir. He ordered a new pack of cards, and I seized the opportunity to cut again, and partnered Sue. She played with automatic dexterity probably born of long practice, but which left you wondering whether she possessed any imagination. We won the first three rubbers.

'Moony!' Caroline screamed for the third time, 'I've passed *twice*.' I doubled and they went down again.

Mounir revoked.

'Moony! You are the limit!'

'Sure am not concentrating.'

The four of us were drinking quite a bit. When you sit with Mounir and accept a whisky, the waiter automatically serves you a new glass as soon as the one you have is empty. The noise from the swimming-pool – you can always detect swimming-pools from a distance, children seem to have a cry peculiar to them – was barely audible in the bridge room. The strong sun outside and the comparative darkness of the room, the coolness, the sort of hush you can hear, and the whisky – everything mingled with beautiful Sue and Caroline – would have been nice and even briefly perfect, if it hadn't been for Caroline giving Mounir hell:

'Moony, you've seen me discard spades *twice* . . .'

'I sure did . . .'

'And then,' she continued, 'you have the cheek, the darned cheek, to lead hearts.'

'I sure . . .' he started, and I burst out laughing.

'I'm glad *you* are enjoying yourself,' she said coldly.

'I am,' I said.

'That's fine.'

'It is.'

There was silence. Even Mounir, intoxicated because he doesn't drink much as a rule, sensed danger. But quite un-expectedly, Caroline smiled and I smiled back and we be-came friends. I tell you, it's strange with American or European women.

'I'll partner Mounir in the next rubber,' I said.

'I hope you can afford it.'

'Fact is, I can't.' Suddenly it pleased me to be poor in that room; I even wished I were genuinely poor and unable to eat enough. But then I wouldn't be in the club, and any-where else but in the club it is very unattractive to be poor.

'I don't believe you,' Caroline said. I insisted on it.

'I'll ask Moony,' she said. 'Moony, is your cousin poor?'

'He sure knows if he needs anything, all he has to do is to ask me.'

We stopped playing while we were speaking and were just about to resume, when a tall, plumpish man in his forties came and put his hands on Caroline's shoulders. He wore spectacles and was bald on top.

'Hiya,' she said, 'working this afternoon?'

'I guess so,' he said. 'We're having trouble with a man called . . . let me see, Abracadabra or something like that.' He looked in his wallet and took a card out. 'I guess we'll have to ask you for help, Moony.' He gave Mounir the card.

'Abdelkerim,' Mounir read. He pronounced it as though to him, too, it was difficult to pronounce. 'I'll fix him.'

'Jack,' Caroline said, 'this is Ram, Moony's cousin.' Jack powerfully shook hands with me and said he was very glad to meet me, and, because I liked him (he looked gentle) I said: 'Glad to meet you too, sir.' Call an American 'sir' and he's half in love with you.

'Are you in the same department as Moony?'

'No, sir.'

'Jack is my husband,' Caroline said.

'Are you working here?' I asked, disappointed because I didn't know the girls were married. Neither wore a ring. 'I thought you were tourists.'

'Jack is on a "fact-finding" mission,' Caroline said.

'Your husband on the same mission too?' I asked Sue. She shook her head. After a while she said: 'I am not married.'

'Sue's my sister,' Jack said. 'Ever since these two girls read *Sinuhe the Egyptian*, they've wanted to come here.'

Mounir called the waiter and Jack ordered a Coca Cola. The score sheets lay neglected on the table, mingled with the playing cards, and any moment now the servant would come and clear the table, throwing the score sheets away.

'What facts,' I asked, absent-mindedly making a neat

136

pack of the cards and retrieving the score sheets, 'are you trying to find, sir?'

'Just call him Jack,' Caroline said.

'Jack,' I said.

'Well,' he said, 'we are a team of people going from one country to another, living *with* the people, the *same way* the people are living, sharing their everyday lives, and finding out what they truly think of the States, and finding out how we can foster and encourage friendship between *us* and *you*.' He pulled up a chair and sat, his face near mine, his hand on the back of my chair; every sentence emphasized neatly and concisely. I remember a pair of American young men belonging to the Mormon sect, who rang at my door in London one day. In the same neat and earnest way, they recited the fact that God is divided into three distinct entities . . . or is it the other way round, I forget which.

'That's very nice,' I said. 'Is this mission government sponsored?'

'Well,' he said, 'indirectly; but we have ourselves formed a committee and have ourselves financed the project.'

'I hope you find it pleasant here,' I said.

'I guess we met with much more hospitality than we reckoned with, and the folks back in the States will be very happy to know we have a large . . . a very large number of friends in this country, Egypt.'

'I'm glad to hear it,' I said.

'Sure met with great kindness,' he said.

I didn't want the conversation to carry away the table; there was this matter of the money I had good on the score sheet.

'Do you play bridge, Jack?' I asked.

'I do,' he said, then: 'That's another bond between our people and you. We have common hobbies, we play the same cards, we speak the same language.'

'Do you play croquet in the States?' I asked.

'Well,' he said, 'I can't say that we do. But there is no reason why we should not.'

'Would be something more in common,' I said.

'Sure would.'

I folded the score sheets, unfolded them, and folded them again. There was this long pause which meant we might all leave the bridge room.

'What's the trouble with this man you just mentioned?' I asked.

'Well, this man Abracadabra,' he smiled broadly at his joke, then suddenly pulled a very straight face, '. . . now don't get me wrong. If I can't pronounce his name it's my own darned fault and I don't mean any disrespect.'

'Of course not,' I said.

'Well, this man is in charge of public relations concerning the President of Egypt; and I would like a photograph of myself shaking the hand of your President.'

I could see the picture, probably the frontispiece of one of the thousands of books in American libraries all over the world, with the caption: The author shaking hands with the President.

'Just leave it to me,' Mounir said.

'Just leave it to Moony,' I repeated. Then I asked him where they were staying, and he said with Moony.

'It must be useful for your fact-findings,' I said, 'to be living with an Egyptian family.'

'It is indeed,' he said, 'my observations are written

down while I am living with the very people I have come to observe.'

'Excellent,' I said. Then I asked him how did the standard of living compare with that in the United States.

'Well,' he said, 'there is a lot of untruth said about this country, Egypt. The folks back home will be surprised when I tell them some of the facts I have accumulated while living here with your cousin and your aunt. Now let me give you a personal example of what I mean.' His eyes wide open, his mouth practically brushing my ear, using his finger for emphasis, he unveiled the accumulated facts gathered whilst living with my cousin and my aunt. 'Back in L.A. where we live,' he continued, 'we have one maid and one cook and no more. My wife Caroline has to do a lot of housework her own self. Well, here the housewife does not do any housework, she has a gardener, a chauffeur, two cooks . . . I believe,' he looked at Mounir for verification, and Mounir nodded wisely, 'and a servant for the house-work.'

'You're doing a fine job, Jack,' I said with an American accent. Then I stood up and said I was going to have a swim and as I might not see them later, I'd better collect this little money I had won at bridge. 'Let me see,' I said. 'That's sixty pounds you've lost, Caroline.' I put the score sheet in front of her.

'Jack, will you give Ram sixty pounds?'

'Sure. Now let me see. How much is that in dollars?' Whereupon Mounir took out his gold pen and calculated how much that was in dollars and then took out his cheque book enclosed in a leather jacket and started writing out a cheque for Sue. Jack gave me two hundred-dollar notes, which is more than sixty pounds but was in accordance with Mounir's gold-pen calculation.

'Anyone else feel like swimming?' I asked, in an attempt on Sue.

'Yes,' Caroline said, standing up. 'See you later.' We walked away together.

'Have you a bathing costume with you?'

She didn't have one. I have a locker in the club containing mine. We stood for a while watching the swimmers. Around the pool people were having lunch and drinking.

'Gee, I do feel like swimming.'

'Don't worry,' I said, 'I'll get you a costume.' I asked her to look at the people around the pool and to tell me if she found a girl of her size. She pointed to a girl reading a book beneath an umbrella.

'I'll be back in a moment,' I said, and walked towards the girl.

'Loula,' I said, 'be a sport and lend me your bathing costume.'

'We were talking about you yesterday, Ram,' she said.

'It doesn't interest me,' I said. 'Anyway I know what you were saying.'

'What?'

'That none of you would marry me.'

'Well, you know what, Ram? Someone said . . .'

'I know, I know; Vicky Doss said she wouldn't mind marrying a penniless man because she's intellectual; and she's intellectual because she lived for two years in her dear Quartier Latin and her St Germain des Prés.'

'*Ouf, tu es antipathique;* anyway, who is the woman with you?'

'An American.' Loula gazed at her.

'*Tu trouves qu'elle est plus jolie que moi?*'

'It doesn't matter,' I said, 'which one of you is more *jolie*; at least she's not a bloody virgin like you.' This kills them. This business of virginity just kills the girls in the club. They're as sophisticated as you could wish, but they are virgins. Even Vicky Doss is a virgin. They remain so until they are married. It kills them.

'*Salaud*,' she said and laughed. 'Here is the key to my locker. She's probably too fat for my costume.' And then, just as I was about to go, she said, 'I hope she doesn't leave anything venereal in my suit.'

'Better,' I said, 'to have loved and to have had a venereal, than never to have loved at all.'

'Perhaps,' she replied, 'but I don't want anything venereal without even having loved.' We both laughed and I went back to Caroline.

After swimming, we had lunch together by the pool. We drank cold Egyptian beer with our steaks and were served by Hassan who had given me the five pounds to play bridge with. Caroline asked me why he was grinning, and I told her about the five pounds.

'I guess you are poor, then.'

'I am,' I said.

'Jack owns two large restaurants in Los Angeles,' she said. 'I was a waitress in one of them.' She too, it seemed, found it nicer to be poor at the moment.

And so, I thought, here we are. We have drunk whisky, we have been sarcastic, we are having lunch by the swimming pool with a beautiful woman, two hundred dollars in our pocket, and Vicky Doss wouldn't say no.

'Where are your thoughts, Ram?'

And then supposing, just supposing, I had never met Edna and had never gone away; would it be so bad marrying Vicky Doss? or Loula who has a sense of humour? and having a beautiful flat and a car, and spending my life in the club, and playing croquet? And even then, even now would it be so bad? Isn't that my real character anyway? A natural son of his upbringing? And for the first time since my return to Egypt I thought of Didi Nackla.

'Gee, you're sighing.'

'Hassan,' I called out. 'Two large cognacs, please.'

'That's a lot we're drinking. You are used to it, I guess?'

'No,' I said.

'My, my,' she said, 'you do look sad.'

I looked at her. We had flirted a bit in the water, I had held her hand and she had squeezed it in response. I took her hand and kissed it.

'You're cute.'

'Thank you,' I said.

Hassan changed one of the hundred-dollar notes, and I had just given him twenty pounds for himself, when Mounir came unsteadily towards us.

'*Seketnalo dechel b'hmaro!*' he shouted in Arabic, which translated would mean: We've put up with so much, he now permits himself to drag his donkey in with him.

'Her husband waiting for her inside, and you having lunch here! *Seketnalo dechel b'hmaro*,' he shouted again.

Our table was placed just next to the pool, and Mounir saw fit to repeat his sentence from that side of the table overlooking the water. He needed just the gentlest of physical persuasions, a tiny little weight to unbalance him.

I gave it. I heard the splash, saw his tie about to follow him in, looked round and ran way. It was too much for me. Coward. Never, I thought, never shall I be Ambassador. Anywhere; not even to an oasis.

I found a taxi just outside the club. I turned to the taxi-driver and asked him how things were with him. He said he wasn't complaining. 'No,' I said, 'I mean since the revolution and all that.'

'I'll tell you,' he said. 'Before the revolution you could only pick up a fare in the posh districts, now the army people also ride in taxis; that means we have the posh people *and* the army,' and as I knew, the army was scattered all over Cairo. No, he said, he wasn't complaining.

'I am glad to hear it,' I said.

'Yes, things are not so bad. Of course one takes what God gives.'

Of course. And if there is no God, nobody gets anything. It's only fair after all. I was a bit drunk.

'You're a good Roman Catholic,' I told him.

'Me? Ha ha. I am named Mohammed after the Prophet.'

'That's what I mean. A good Moslem Roman Catholic.'

'I bet you've had a bit,' he said.

'Me? No.'

'Very difficult to get now,' he said.

'I know.'

'Very expensive,' he said.

'Yes.'

'Still, if you feel like it, you know; I mean if you're in the mood; it's just possible . . .'

'No,' I said.

'Pure stuff. The same we used to get before the revolution.'

'No,' I said. I wasn't interested. I've often smoked hashish, but never alone, and I never go out of my way to procure it. Still, it is there if one wants it.

I put my hand in my pocket to pay him, and grasped this wad of money I had forgotten all about. It cheered me up.

I went upstairs to the snooker club and asked Font if he'd like to play snooker.

'No,' he said, 'I have to go shopping. Look after the place until I come back.'

I went downstairs to the shoe-store and asked Varenian if he wanted to have a game of snooker with me.

'What are you playing for, excellence?'

'A pound a point,' I said.

'*Andiamo*,' he shouted. We were just about to go upstairs, when Doromian came running from the back room. There followed one of those loud and passionate conversations in Armenian I love hearing. Doromian starts a tirade and carries it higher and higher until he has reached the top of his pitch, at which point Varenian comes to his rescue, carries the conversation downwards to a sonorous plea for generosity and a final appeal with his hands, his four fingers touching the tip of his thumb and his arm outstretched. Then, after mixing modulations for a few minutes in a cacophony of funny-sounding words, there is silence, each utters one syllable, and they are agreed. They toss up. It is Doromian, after all, who'll play with me, and not Varenian. But that is not all. Doromian insists he has also bet a pound he'd win the toss, while Varenian pretends that not at all, it has been decided that the winner will give the loser one pound as a consolation prize. However, it is only one pound and Varenian admits he was only joking. They insult each other in a friendly way, Varenian makes a few obscene gestures and noises, and finally Doromian and myself go upstairs.

'The professor forming a government?' Doromian asked.

'Gone shopping,' I said, setting the balls on the table.

'Guillotines, no doubt.'

'Yes.'

He took his jacket off, put the ends of his tie between shirt and body, and practised some shots on another table.

'In which university have you learnt snooker?' he asked.

'In Turkey,' I said.

There is a group of Turkish members in the snooker club with whom Doromian and Varenian brandish macabre jokes when playing.

'Allah,' says a Turk, 'you'd have made a beautiful sausage, you would have. I've just received a box of Lokoum from Ankara, smells just like you. The fat comes from mother Doromian, my grandfather had her melted at home.'

'My mother is at home,' Doromian says. 'She was constipated for a long time until we built her a little mosque in our flat – she was so used to using them for such matters in Turkey.'

'Your money, excellence,' Doromian now said.

I took the wad of notes out of my pocket and placed it on the window-sill. He also took a bundle of pound notes and placed it next to mine. Then he chalked his cue, scrutinized the tip, crossed himself, murmuring something in Armenian, and made an 'X' sign on the table with his finger to bring me bad luck.

'You start,' he said.

'No,' I said, 'you start.'

It is impossible to score with the first shot because the balls are still grouped together.

'Copt,' he said, spitting in his hanky. He sat down, pretending no more interest in the game, and I did likewise, placing my snooker stick in its stand and looking out of the window. Suddenly I pretended to see Varenian from the window and gesticulated wildly, inviting him to come up for a game.

'Bashooving!' (or something like that) shouted Doromian, running to the window. 'We'll toss up.'

'All right,' I said.

He won the toss and I started. Half-way through the game Font returned.

'What are you playing for,' he asked.

'Pound a point.' He looked at the score; I was forty points to the good.

'Will you make some Bass, Font?'

'Bass, Bass,' mimicked Doromian, who was annoyed about the forty points. 'Why don't you call it beer like everyone else?'

'Bass is the beer of the intellectuals,' I said.

'I beg your pardon, I beg your pardon,' he said, bowing down to the floor. 'I haven't read your latest book,' he said to Font, 'will it be translated in Armenian?'

'Of course you've learnt the alphabet,' I told Doromian.

'Yes', he said, 'and I hope the professor will not mix it up in his book.'

I laughed. Font sat on the window-sill watching the game.

'I am losing forty pounds,' Doromian told Font, 'and I

want to write a thesis about not playing snooker with Copts who pretend they are drunk. Zazmadarian Doromian, *Docteur ès-snooker à votre service.*' He came to Font and bowed down once more. Extending one hand behind him, thinking I didn't notice, he moved the black ball, worth seven points, i.e. seven pounds, to just in front of a pocket. However, before you are allowed to shoot the black, you have to pocket a red ball. There was a red ball conveniently pocketable for Doromian – which I moved when he moved the black.

'And now,' said Doromian, chalking his cue once more, 'Grock, the private clown of the professor . . .' He then noticed the red ball had changed positions. He stood very still, then sat on a leather armchair, staring at me.

'You've changed the position of a red ball,' he said, pointing his finger at me.

'Yes,' I said.

He appealed to Font. 'I have never been to university,' he said, 'I have no degrees. I went to a humble school, and I am a poor man. But never would I cheat. No,' he said, shaking his head. 'Never.'

Font stared at me. 'Ram, have you cheated?'

'Yes,' I said.

Just next to Font, where he was sitting, were the bundles of money. Font took them both and gave them to Doromian. Doromian put them in his pocket and put his jacket on. I remained sitting. He went towards the exit door and looked at me. I didn't move.

'Dirty Egyptian,' he laughed. 'In Farouk's time I'd have done it, but now I'm scared.' He gave me my wad of notes, paid the forty pounds he had so far lost, and placed the black ball in its original position. I put the red where it had been and we continued the game. Twenty minutes later it ended. He gave me another thirty pounds which he had lost, and went out cursing my luck in Armenian. I locked the door behind him.

'Font,' I said. 'Do you really think I would cheat?'

'Yes,' he said.

We had quarrelled many times since my return, and it always meant two or three weeks of not going to the snooker club.

'You know what you're like?' I said. 'You're like a man who buys a valveless radio because he likes silence.'

'What do you mean?'

'Work it out for yourself.'

'What . . .'

'I mean what the bloody hell do you think you're doing; working like a bloody fool here and passing lofty judgments on me. Why the hell don't you pull yourself together and get yourself a decent job and . . .'

'You can talk,' he said. 'What are *you* doing?'

'I'm not talking about myself,' I said.

'Why don't *you* get a job?'

'It so happens,' I shouted, 'that I do have a job . . .'

'What?'

'Never mind,' I said, annoyed that I had started to quarrel with him again. He pretended to be busy putting the snooker balls away.

If he did get a job, that is, without being 'placed' somewhere or other by my aunt or someone like her, he'd earn about twenty pounds a month which is what Jameel now gives him. We have an amazing amount of engineers, lawyers, architects, chemists, physicists who are either jobless or earning twenty pounds in government employment, sitting behind desks doing nothing all day long. They get excellent offers of jobs from South America, Sudan, Ghana, Turkey and even Germany; but they are not given passports and are not allowed to leave. I can't understand why. They are jobless. That, however, is not why Font doesn't work.

'Font,' I said quietly, 'what is it exactly you want?'

'Oh, shut up,' he said. As I said before, he doesn't know what he wants. I went behind the bar and started mixing some Bass. It was Font's afternoon off and he locked all the doors.

'There,' I said, giving him his beer-mug full of Bass. 'Font,' I asked, 'do you know who did this terrible thing to Edna?'

He shook his head.

'God,' I said, 'I'd murder whoever did it.'

'You,' Font sneered. 'You even stayed in England while the English were bombarding Port Said.'

'Much good it did, you coming back,' I said. 'Yehia was in Paris having a holiday,' I continued, 'he didn't come back either. Why don't you sneer at him as you do at me?'

'Yehia,' he repeated. 'Are you like Yehia?'

'No,' I sighed, 'I'm an intellectual like you.'

And then there could have started one of these repartees I am tired and weary of; those shovels of mud which only help to bury the old Font and the old me in our suspended graves. Suspended between eras of civilization. 'I never said I'm an intellectual.' 'No, but you think you are . . .'

I changed the subject.

'Let's have a game of snooker, Font.'

'What's this job you say you do?' he asked after a while.

I belong to a secret organization the head of which is Dr Hamza, Jameel's father. He is collecting documents, pictures and literature, concerning atrocities carried out in our political prisons and concentration camps. He is the type: as I said earlier, a French-educated intellectual of *les droits de l' homme* beliefs, he is compiling a *dossier* about these things which he intends to present to the United Nations. The strange thing about these prisons and camps is that the rich landowners and reactionaries who still favour a régime like that of Farouk, are well treated, allowed special privileges and given lenient sentences. The others, though, the communists, the pacifists and those who see no economic future unless a peace is arranged with Israel, are tortured and terribly ill-treated. The trouble with Dr Hamza is that although he already has more than enough material for his purpose, he keeps putting off presenting it, or carrying out whatever his plan is.

I drive once a week to those places to visit police officers supposed to be friends of mine. They hand me an envelope containing pictures and reports written by the inmates and in return I pay them a certain sum of money. I have the terrible feeling that some of the pictures wouldn't be so gory if we didn't pay for them.

This is all I do.

'What's this job?' Font asked again.

'Nothing,' I told him.

I have never wanted anything tragic to touch me, to afflict me. I don't even want to see anything tragic. And yet, since . . . well, since London and all that, I always seem to move towards the tragic things, as though I had no free will of my own. It is funny how people – millions and millions of people – go about watching the telly and singing and humming in spite of the fact that they lost brother or father or lover in a war; and what is stranger still, they contemplate with equanimity seeing their other brothers or lovers off to yet another war. They don't see the tragedy of it all. Now and then one of the millions reads a book, or starts thinking, or something shakes him, and then he sees tragedy all over the place. Wherever he looks, he finds tragedy. He finds it tragic that other people don't see this tragedy around them and then he becomes like Font or Edna, or joins some party or other, or marches behind banners until his own life, seen detachedly, becomes a little tragic. I hate tragedy.

'Nothing,' I repeated. 'Come, Font, let's have a game.' Sometimes we still have a quiet, friendly game, Font and I. Not for money or anything like that; just friendly and sarcastic about each other's game.

'Got anything to eat in the kitchen, Font?'

'Yes. Make some more Bass and I'll get something.'

He went into the kitchen and came back with a tray full of little plates; hazel-nuts, peanuts, pickled onions, white cheese, celery stuck in beer glasses. The Bass had put us in a better mood.

'Cheers, Font.'

'Cheers, Ram.'

Font switched on the light over the snooker table, we rolled our sleeves up, chose sticks, rubbed the ends with chalk and powdered our hands. The rest of the hall was dark and cool because Font had closed all the shutters, and that oblong light reflected on the green table with the coloured balls was nice to look at.

Font hit the triangle and all the reds dispersed.

'You're a good shot,' I said. 'Another yard to the left and you might have pocketed something.'

I tried to pocket a comparatively easy red, but missed. Font said he'd see about ordering a snooker table with larger pockets for me. We were just getting into our stride, so to speak, when we heard loud voices and bangs on the door.

'Police—open up!'

'*Kyria lysoon*,' I said. I don't know what *Kyria lysoon* is, neither does Font, but we have often heard high Coptic priests sing it in the churches of Egypt. There they stand under their magnificent beards and sing what sounds like *Kyria lysoon* to four ugly, orthodox youths, who sing *Kyria lysoon* back to them. Long ago Font and I came to the conclusion this was a secret tennis match being played between the priest and the youths, with *Kyria lysoon* for balls. Font got a tummy cramp once, laughing. The priest serves a *Kyria lysoon* and you can see the four youths bumping each other trying to hit it back to him. They often miss, and a *Kyria lysoon* is heard bouncing in a corner of the church. But that particular priest was a fantastic player. He used to take a *Kyria lysoon* from the youths before they even served it as it were, modulating it cunningly in his own corner, and before you knew where you were, he had a smasher right out of the window, the youths looking at each other in perplexity. Once the priest came to speak to us after church and Font said: 'Well played, sir,' in English. I nearly died laughing.

I don't know why I suddenly said *Kyria Iysoon* when I heard 'police' at the door. Perhaps because my religion never went further than laughing at *Kyria Iysoon*, and because one looks to God when in fear.

I caught Font's head and covered his mouth with my hand.

'Listen,' I whispered, 'you don't know where I am.' I let him go. 'Take your time opening the door. Give me time to jump from the window.' I was trembling.

'Open up! Open up, Font, you rascal. Look what we've got.'

I recognized Jameel and Fawzi's voices. I sat down wiping the sweat off my face. I went behind the bar and poured myself a large cognac. Font opened the door.

'We've got a present for you, Font,' they shouted. They were drunk. They had three Greek prostitutes with them. I recognized one of them, called Ellena; she sits at the bar of the Hotel de Paris. They caught Font and danced ringa-ringa-roses with him. The girls were also drunk. One of them lay on a snooker table and pulled her skirt up, while another took a snooker stick and pretended to be an impatient man. Jameel saw me and ran towards me: 'Ramos – Ramos.' He took a bottle from behind the bar and went to the girls.

I sat on a stool and poured myself another cognac. It was the first time in my life I had experienced real fear. Terror. It was like a fantastic smack on the face. It was as though I had been drunk all my life and had suddenly sobered up.

'Ram.'

'Yes.'

'What's the matter with you?'

'Nothing.'

'Your hand is shaking.'

'The Bass has turned my stomach somehow. I wanted to vomit.'

Font sat gazing at me, his eyebrows high up in his forehead.

'Why did you want to run away when you heard the word "police"?'

'Run away? I was only joking; pretending they were real police and that they were after me.'

He kept on staring at me. Sometimes your emotions are unexpectedly stirred and you suddenly become angry or sentimental or sad. I wanted to pat Font on the back.

'Why don't you take one of the girls to your room, Font?'

'Ram,' he said. 'Are you involved in some organization or something dangerous?'

'No.'

'Ram, are you a member of the Communist Party?'

I laughed.

'Ram . . .'

'Font, take Ellena and go home.' I took a bundle of notes out of my pocket. 'Take Ellena and have a good time. Take a bottle with you. Go on, Font. I know you haven't had a woman for months.'

He wants to go, but he is shy. In England Font could share both his ideals and his body with someone of the opposite sex; but here it is impossible.

I poured him a cognac.

Times like this must drive him mad, thinking of Brenda Dungate in London. There was talk of marriage between them. The Suez war put a stop to all that.

I had calmed down and began to regain my old self. Jameel was in the kitchen with a girl and Fawzi was sleeping in an armchair. Ellena and the other girl were eating from the tray and drinking cognac from the bottle.

This Ellena. I used to know her as a child. She is the daughter of one of the dressmakers my mother and aunts used to go to. When young I used to go with my mother to those dressmakers; Greek, Armenian, Maltese, sometimes French. Always the same. A threadbare room with a sewing machine and pins and pieces of cloth and thread all over the place; also a large horse-shoe magnet. Maria or Talma or Juno or Georgette of whatever that particular dressmaker's name was, would have about four children, pale little things playing on the floor. The dressmakers had sidelines such as making halawa, which is a sticky paste made of lemon and sugar and used for peeling hair off the body. They also knew secrets such as how to beget boys and not girls, or girls and not boys, or none at all. And while my mother wriggled in and out of dresses or screamed and shrieked because of the halawa, I used to pick things up with the magnet.

'Where is your father?' I asked Ellena once, trying to pick up scissors with the magnet.

'Which one?'

'What do you mean, which one?' I asked. 'Your father.'

'I have many fathers,' she replied.

'Is that so?' I said, astonished, finally picking up the scissors.

Another time after school, I went to her mother, Camille — I remember her name — for a dress of my mother's.

'How many fathers have *you*?' Ellena asked.

'None,' I said, 'but I have four mothers.'

'Silly!'

'I have four mothers,' I said. 'What are you going to be when you grow up?'

'Dressmaker, and you?'

'I don't know. A jockey perhaps.' I decided I wanted to be a jockey and started riding the sofa's arm and whipping it.

'Come, I'll show you something,' she said.

I followed her behind a curtain where she took her underpants off and raised her skirt.

I looked at her and touched her with the magnet, then went home.

I looked at Ellena now, swinging the bottle of cognac to her lips. She hadn't yet seen me. When she does, she will bend her head and shake hands with me: 'Monsieur Ram,' she will say, embarrassed and ashamed.

Font was looking at Ellena in the mirror behind the bar. There is something in the warm Egyptian afternoon which is torture to young men. I have known those terrible yearnings, too. After school, at two in the afternoon, just finished eating, my mother in her room, the flat darkened, there would be this buzz of heat in our ears and we would lie, Font and I, each in his bed, tossing. The warm, white sheets and the near-feverish body, sensual and uncomfortable, as instinctively we tried to find a cool place in the bed. The stomach would be satiated with food and we would know a profound yearning for a woman's body to share this damp sultriness. If we were lucky, we fell asleep.

'How much money have you got, Font?'

'Fifteen piastres.' We would count our money, usually borrowing something at fantastic interest from Corollos,

156

who knew why we wanted it, then tiptoe by my mother's room. Suddenly: '*Qu'est-ce que tu fais?*'

'*Rien.*' She also would be tossing, the miserable widow, still in her thirties. Perhaps we had woken her, and to awaken someone in the Egyptian afternoon is a terrible thing. A scene would take place: 'You are inconsiderate' – 'What have I done?' – 'You are selfish' – 'Why?' – 'I can't go back to sleep' – 'I didn't know you were sleeping' – 'What do you want anyway?' – 'Nothing.' I would slip the car-keys in my pocket because I was too young to take the car. And then downstairs Font and I. 'I'll drive' – 'No, I'll drive' – 'No, I'll drive' – 'All right, you drive.' And when that was settled, the cramp in the stomach just as when entering the examination hall. Then the hours'-long search. 'Here, here is one' – 'No, that's the one wouldn't come' – 'No, it's another one' – 'All right': but by the time we had reversed, another car would have stopped and picked her up. We would search again, in all the little streets and alleys where they ought to be; but it would be early in the afternoon and a bad time; although early in the afternoon was the time we wanted it most. And if it did happen, she'd say twenty piastres, and we'd say yes and she'd say where, and we'd say in the car. Driving feverishly towards the desert. Hot. Sticky. One of us leaves the car, comes back ten minutes later – it never lasts longer. The other one leaves the car. Back at home we would be disappointed and frustrated. Nothing as voluptuous as our thoughts. When we had grown a bit, we went with the married women in the club, but Font doesn't go to the club any more.

I had recovered completely from that short panic I experienced when hearing the word 'police'. I wanted to go home for a bath and change of clothes, but kept putting off seeing my mother.

The telephone rang and Font went to answer.

I wanted to sit somewhere alone and nice where I could think. I thought of Edna and my hand went to the bottle of cognac. But I stopped myself.

'It's your mother,' Font said. 'She says you're to go home at once. Your aunt is there, and your uncle Amis is arriving any moment from Upper Egypt.'

'Jesus,' I said, 'I pushed Mounir in the swimming pool yesterday and I shall never hear the end of it.'

I left the bundle of notes on the bar for Font and took a taxi home.

PART IV

'*Il faut qu'il se marie,*' my aunt was saying, 'Enough is enough.'

'I have done all I can,' my mother said. 'I have sacri . . .'

'. . . ficed my life for him.' I finished her sentence.

'No, no, no,' my uncle, the Pasha said. 'More respect, more respect.'

They sat there discussing me. This business of pushing Mounir in the pool would never end, it seemed. The Pasha, one of our few surviving male relatives, lives in Upper Egypt looking after the land. As each aunt lost her husband, or each cousin his parents, the Pasha liquidated his assets and bought land near where he lived. He is the only one amongst us not westernized, and I would like him, if only it weren't for the infuriating respect he pays to the 'educated' part of the family. Originally we had about four Pashas in the family, but as they all died early, my aunts put their heads together and it was decided to buy a title for this one. It cost thirty-five thousand pounds, and this is how it was done: a cheap plot of land was bought and converted into a park, and it was then announced that my uncle was giving the park away to the public. Ministers were invited for the giving-away ceremony and my aunts and their influential friends acted as hosts at the party which followed. The plot of land and its conversion had cost one thousand pounds. The other thirty-four thousand pounds . . . well, never mind; just the other thirty-four thousand pounds. Two days later Farouk announced my uncle a Pasha. He is illiterate, my uncle. Three years after that the revolution took place and titles were abolished, but all those who were Pashas are still called Pasha.

Well, the Pasha had been called from Upper Egypt. Oh,

not because I had pushed Mounir in the pool, but because the said Mounir wants to buy a villa in Heliopolis and they wonder if an extra thirty thousand pounds or so could be squeezed out of the fellah without actually selling any land.

I looked at my uncle and winked. He shook his head violently. And then the whole business started again.

'It *was* an accident,' I said.

'Certainly not. You did it on purpose.'

My mother took her handkerchief out of her bag, and tears rolled down her cheeks. Suddenly she looked round, opened her crumpled handkerchief quite flat, as though showing us there was nothing in it, and blew her nose.

I laughed out loud. My mother has a reputation for crocodile tears. She used to put a piece of onion in her handkerchief, until the sudden reek made me suspicious one day.

'What are you laughing at?' my aunt shouted.

'Honestly, honestly,' I said; 'I just tried to get out of my chair and accidentally knocked against him.'

'Liar! Why did you run away then?'

'I've explained a thousand times.' My explanation was that Mounir was so popular at the club and myself so un-popular, I was afraid the servants would have thrown me out themselves. This pleases her. But she was still threaten-ing to take my mother to live with her and to give our flat up.

'Give him another chance,' said my uncle the Pasha.

'Pasha, he is not normal.'

Sometimes my humour-nerve or sympathetic-nerve or whatever you want to call it, is unexplainably stretched and even the softest breeze, as it were, can make it tingle. Again I laughed. It's this word 'Pasha' you see. My uncle's name is Amis, and they called him Amis until titles were abolished. Suddenly, for thirty-five thousand pounds' worth, they call him Pasha. I couldn't.control myself.

'*Regarde-le . . .*'

'I'm sorry,' I said. 'I'm just tired. I have a little bit of fever.'

My mother sprang out of her chair with her hand stretched straight to my forehead.

'*Il est brûlant,*' she screamed. *C'est peut être la typhoïde.*'

'*La typhoïde,* to us, has a value all its own. It is used, like the gambler's fare home, only when everything else is lost. It will surprise the medical profession to know that in our families various people have had typhoid many times. We love that disease, but although we love it, we don't like to die of it (as many of us have). Hence the blessing of chloro-mycin. We can now have typhoid without actually dying. The disease is endowed with ceremonies, blessings and rituals accompanying the survivor long after his recovery. As I said, many of us *have* died of it, and so it hasn't lost its power for attracting solicitude, affection and money, chloromycin or not.

'Really,' my aunt said, 'he's already had it twice.'

'*Je t'en prie,*' my mother said. 'Ziza had it twice and died of it the third time.'

I didn't particularly want *la typhoïde* then. The last time I had it, Font was living with us and I persuaded him to have it too because we were both unprepared for our exams. Our professor relative, the university lecturer, decided we were too weak to study, and so hinted at our coming questions –

hinted, that is, by giving us the actual papers two weeks before we were due to see them. As my mother had said then, through an aromatic tear, 'they probably won't live to see the results.'

No, I didn't want *la typhoïde*. I was thinking of this, when I heard the word *armée*.

The army, our army. The one which travels in taxis. It is surprising how, during my sojourn in London, my family had become reconciled to the army. Not only reconciled to it, but actually getting in to it. Soon, one could see, we were going to *be* the army. Cousins, relatives, brothers were being snatched from the universities and placed in the army. Although 'don't you know who I am – I am a Pasha or the son of one', has not quite been dropped, it is quite fashionable now to say: 'Don't you know who I am – I am a colonel or a general or the son of one.' They want me to get into the army.

'The best people,' my aunt was saying, 'are in it. Don't think,' she continued, 'it is the shabby affair it was. Are you better than Safwat, the son of Boulos Pasha?'

'I am not,' I said.

'. . . or than Ammoon and his brother Yassa?'

'I am particularly worse than they,' I said.

'. . . or than the son of Foufou?'

'No,' I said.

'Or . . .'

'It is decided,' my mother said. 'You are to go into the army and get married.'

'Yes,' I said.

'After all, I have sacr . . .'

'. . . ificed your life for me.'

'A good girl from a good family,' my uncle, the Pasha, said.

'Yes,' I said, 'with a little bit of land.'

'Yes,' he said.

'And something in the bank.'

'Would do no harm . . .'

'Preferably of military background,' I said. This annoys him somewhat. The fellah is not as terror-stricken at the word Pasha as he is now at the word Officer.

'*Tu as fini?*' my aunt said.

'Yes.'

'Because if you haven't quite finished,' she said, 'I shall close your mouth for good.'

I shut up.

'Om Kalsoom is singing on the radio,' I told my uncle.

'*Voilà!*' shouted my aunt. 'That's all he's good for. Anything to annoy us.'

From Turkey to North Africa, Om Kalsoom is the most beloved and revered person alive. She cuts across all sections of the people. A woman in her forties now, she has led an irreproachable life and she possesses a voice of heart-rending simplicity and beauty.

'What . . . what is she singing?' my uncle asked, starting to fidget.

'*Voilà,*' my aunt repeated.

'*Sing to me slowly, slowly,*' I told him. Her songs last for hours. But those of the French *pensionnat*, the club and the 'travelled' consider it a sign of commonness to appreciate Om Kalsoom. Because they are nevertheless oriental musically, they listen instead to Madam Amalia Rodriguez of Portugal, who very feebly resembles Om Kalsoom in voice.

'Her best song,' my uncle sighed.

'This is intolerable,' my aunt said. 'This is the limit.'

'What have I done?' I said.

'Do you want us to sit for hours listening to those wails?' she screamed.

'I didn't know you didn't like her,' I said.

'Switch the radio on very softly,' she said, controlling herself, 'and don't utter another word.'

I switched the radio on and returned to my seat, folding my arms. I pretended not to notice my uncle who had pulled his chair up to the radio, stuck his ear to the loud-speaker, and was looking miserable.

'Put it on louder,' she screamed, '*nom de Dieu!*'

I turned the knob until the music was audible and returned to my seat.

Corrollos, the servant, stood at the doorway listening. He wears an even more pathetic expression when my aunt visits us.

'Get a chair from the kitchen and sit down,' my aunt told him. He looked at her with indescribable devotion, managed to make his eyes water, and returned to the kitchen.

'*Pauvre type,*' my aunt said.

'I don't know that I can afford to keep him any longer,' my mother said.

My aunt grunted.

'I haven't had a new dress for years. That's how I live now,' my mother continued. Two days before she had bought two new dresses.

'First the car, and now the servants. God knows how it will end.'

'Yes,' I said, 'it's terrible.'

'It's all because of you,' she said, taking her handkerchief out again.

'Now, now, now,' my uncle said. 'You're a good boy, Ram. Don't make your mother unhappy.'

'I am sorry,' I told my uncle. 'Would you like a cigarette, Uncle Amis?'

'Yes,' he said, staring at me. 'I'll try one of yours.'

I took my pack out and went to him. I pointed to a particular cigarette and whispered he should smoke it in the bathroom. He nodded eagerly and left. Two minutes later he returned with a disappointed look on his face. I laughed out loud.

'But he's completely mad,' my aunt said.

'I am sorry,' I said again. 'I shan't utter another word.' My uncle had thought the cigarette was stuffed with hashish.

Corrollos returned again, standing within sight of my aunt, and thinking I didn't notice him.

'Miserable beggar,' my aunt said. 'Get a chair and sit down, Corrollos. Sit down until the song is ended.' He shook his head and returned to the kitchen.

I followed him.

'Leave him alone,' my mother said.

I closed the kitchen door and sat on the gas-oven looking at Corrollos.

'Where is the radio I gave you?' I asked.

He shook his head.

'By God, I'll murder you,' I said. 'Where is it?'

'I don't know how to use it,' he whined.

'You've been using it for a year.'

'I'm afraid to break it.'

'Put it on the table,' I said, 'and switch it on.'

He got it out of the kitchen cupboard, put it on the table, and switched it on without plugging it in, shaking his head all the while and handling it as though it were a crystal chandelier.

'It's silent,' I told him.

He bent his head to the loud-speaker and listened intently.

'Well?'

He shook his head again.

'You've broken it,' I told him. 'I am going to deduct two pounds from your salary.' I pretended I was leaving the kitchen.

'Perhaps I forgot to plug it,' he said.

'Perhaps,' I said.

He plugged it.

'What's this theatre you play every time my aunt comes here?' I asked.

'What theatre?'

'Don't you know? Did she ever give you a tip in her life, you bloody swine?'

Tip? What tip? He starts whining and tears actually flow down his cheeks and because he has no handkerchief he makes a mess of the tip of his robe.

I left him and returned to the sitting-room.

'I do all I can,' my uncle was saying, 'but they don't pay.'

'How long do we have to put up with all this?' my aunt asked.

'They don't pay,' repeated my uncle. 'They haven't got the money.'

'Haven't got the money,' snorted my aunt. I'd rather let the land lie idle than have them rob us in this way.'

Egyptian landowners usually let the land to tenants and do not bother to cultivate it themselves.

'That would be worse still,' my uncle said. 'The land would go bad and we'd get a bad name in the district.'

'Bad name,' mimicked my aunt.

'The times are hard,' said my uncle.

'You're too good to them,' she said. 'That's what's wrong with you. You've spoiled them.'

'The times have changed,' he said.

'You'll have to do something. Mounir will be getting married soon.'

'We shall have to sell,' he said.

'Sell-sell-sell,' she shouted. 'If they have the money to buy, they can pay the rent.'

'It's not they that buy, my sister,' he said. 'Sell one of the apartment houses in Cairo.'

'Do you think I am mad? That's what we've come to. We starve while the fellaheen owe us money.'

He is kind and gentle, my Uncle Amis, and like any other animal bloats himself on what is within his reach without thinking of anything in particular. Even the fallaheen love him because he sits with them and cracks jokes. He even weeps at their misery at times, just like them, without searching for the cause of that misery. 'The world,' he sighs, and they sigh with him and repeat: 'The world.'

'Who's starving?' I asked.

'What?' she shouted. 'Vivi,' she said, turning to my mother, 'I can't bear to see your son any more. I'll have a nervous breakdown.'

'I don't know what to do with him,' my mother cried.

'But I know,' said my aunt. 'You are going to live with me and give this flat up. We shall see what he will do then.'

My mother started crying now, in earnest.

'Apologize to your aunt, Ram, apologize,' my uncle said.

'I am sorry,' I said.

'Go and kiss her hand,' he said.

'*Surtout pas!*' she screamed.

I made as though to go towards her, when the door bell rang. It was Marie. She made straight for my uncle.

'Pasha,' she screamed in Arabic, 'how wonderful to see you again. I have always been asking about you. You look very well indeed.' Then she turned round to my aunt and said: '*Il a l'air malade, le pauvre.*'

My uncle is always very embarrassed when society showers it charm upon him for a few seconds. He mumbled polite formulas in Arabic, smiled awkwardly and didn't know what to do with his hands.

'Vivi,' Marie turned to my mother, and then saw she was crying. 'Poor Vivi,' she said, changing her tone. 'You've always had trouble, Vivi *cherie*.' She patted her on the back, kissed my aunt on both cheeks, took her gloves off, and sat down.

'Good afternoon,' I said.

'Didn't I say *bonjour* to you?'

'No,' I said.

'What an afternoon,' she said. 'I can't think clearly any more.'

'Tell us what happened,' I said, in a conversational tone.

Marie has always been afraid of me. I don't know why.

She is one of those devout Catholics who used to go about calling everyone *cousine* and *petite sœur*, and had reached her forties without getting married. She continued to call everyone *tante* and *oncle*, jumping up to kiss them, wearing masculine-type shoes with flat soles, until my aunt suddenly took her under her wing. '*Elle est tellement serviable, cette Marie*,' and told her at once not to call her *tante* and to put a stop to all the kid-play.

Marie now looked at my aunt, who made a 'don't bother about him' sign with her head.

'I hope you are keeping well, Madame Marie,' my uncle said, 'madame' being his epitome of sophistication.

'*Comme il est gentil*,' she said. 'Thank you very much, Pasha. Here we are living from day to day, not knowing what will happen next.'

He murmured appropriate condolences.

'*Je me demande*,' she told my aunt, 'how he can live in that village all the time.'

'Thank God he remained a fellah,' my aunt said. 'Can you see me dealing with those people there?'

'You must come to Cairo more often,' Marie said, raising her voice somewhat as is the habit with people who think the other person doesn't speak the language.

He thanked her profusely.

I left them and went to bed. I lay on my back with my hands joined beneath my head. I had reached an impasse again; a cul-de-sac. Again I didn't know what to do with myself. Seeing Edna again after such a long time; and now that scar of hers. I sighed.

Our love had always been mingled with politics. From

the very day I had met her at my aunt's, politics had something to do with our love. *Un amour*, like literature, *engagé*.
I laughed.

Two hours later, when my aunt had left, the Pasha came
into my room. I pretended to be asleep.

'Come, come, you rascal, you are not asleep.'

I snored.

'Look, look what I have.'

I didn't move. I heard him fumbling with papers in his
pocket.

'Ahem,' he said, 'would you like to see . . .'

I sprang out of bed and snatched an envelope from his
hand.

'Ram—Ram. No, no. Be fair, be honest.'

'So, you swine,' I said. 'Kah kah kah,' I cackled like a
hen. 'You are going to spend a nice quiet evening with your
sisters, you are.'

'No, no, no, Ram. First give me back that envelope.' He
tried to snatch it, then sat down panting. I sat on the bed
and opened it. They were hundred-pound notes. I counted
fifteen.

'I am not speaking to you,' I said.

'My God, what have I done?'

'Siding with the others.'

'No, no, no,' he said. 'Just for form; just for form. Do
you think I understand those foreign words they use? First
give me back the money.'

'Anyway,' I said, 'I am not taking you out tonight.'

'Is this the way you treat your Uncle Amis?—your poor
Uncle Amis who hasn't been to town for a whole year? Is

this the way? Your Uncle Amis who paid four hundred pounds for you which you lost gambling?'

'What?'

'I swear by the Virgin Mary; I paid it for you. Here, look.' He took a receipt from his wallet and gave it to me, snatching the money from my hand as he did so.

Six months earlier I had lost four hundred pounds playing baccarat and had given an I.O.U.

'You're a king, you are,' I told him. 'You'll have a wonderful time tonight. Don't worry. My sweet fellah of an uncle. The nectar of the Gods you are . . . if only you'd treat the fellah a little better . . .'

'Na na na na,' he said. 'Ram, don't start with all this nonsense.'

'All right,' I said.

'Come now,' he said, pulling me from the bed. 'To the telephone.'

'First tell me what you want.'

'First,' he said, 'a game of poker until the evening. Then . . . where is the place with the red-headed bellydancer? And then . . .'

I went to the telephone.

'Jameel? Uncle Amis is in town.'

'*Amuse-le, le pauvre,*' my mother said as we left.

I felt terrible when I awoke in the morning. I was sleeping in the sitting-room because my uncle occupied my room. We had smoked hashish the night before, and the memory of our vulgar orgy at the snooker club gave me nausea. He had spent six hundred pounds, my uncle. The red-headed dancer, three of her troupe and her flautist had been brought to the snooker club. Omar and Yehia had also been there. Ellena, too, and the other two prostitutes. I gave an involuntary groan. Font had started to cry suddenly amidst this dissipation, and to keep him company, Ellena had cried too. My uncle had collapsed at about three o'clock and Jameel ran into a lamp-post driving us home. The seven of us carried my uncle up to bed.

I opened my eyes. My mother was sitting darning my socks. She wears glasses when she does that; and when she wears glasses her appearance is completely transformed. As though in harmony with her appearance, which is intelligent and intent, she becomes more reflective and quiet.

'*Tu souffres?*' she asked.

'A bit of a headache and a thick head. It was terrible yesterday. Your brother is horribly vulgar.'

'What do you expect? Still a bachelor at his age and he only comes to town once a year. Besides, he never had our education.'

'No,' I sighed.

'Have a cup of coffee. There is some warm croissant, too.' She poured me a cup and gave me a croissant. Very rarely, we arrive at a son-mother intimacy, and when it happens, it is always in the morning when I wake up.

'Don't smoke yet. Eat something first.'

'All right,' I said.

She went on with her darning.

'Dr Hamza telephoned twice yesterday,' she said.

'Yes?'

'*Il est très aristocrate, cet homme; tiens,* he's the uncle of Didi Nackla. *Elle est adorable, cette fille.* Mounir will be very happy with her. She is also very lucky to get him.'

'Are they going to get married, then?' It surprised me. Mounir was not Didi's type.

'Yes. Your aunt is arranging everything. *Ça sera un couple charmant.*'

'Yes,' I said.

'She was in England, wasn't she?'

'For a while,' I said.

'Did you often see her?'

'She lived with us.'

'*Pas possible!* You never told me about that.'

'No,' I said.

'*Comment?* She lived with you and Font?'

'And Edna,' I said.

'It must have been wonderful, Ram. Don't think I don't realize it must be hard for you being poor.' She sighed. *Les beaux voyages*, she continued, which she used to make every year. Dancing the Charleston the whole night. And then Paris, Josephine Baker, Maurice Chevalier, even Maxim's, Ram dear. The best hotels only. *Tout le monde me faisaient la cour.* And now . . .

'I wonder why he telephoned?' she asked after a while.

'Who?'

'Dr Hamza.'

'Probably something to do with Jameel,' I said. 'Levy is giving him Arabic lessons.'

'*A propos,*' my mother said; 'your aunt wants Levy to brush up Mounir's Arabic. You must give me his address. It was terrible what you did, darling. Why did you push him in the water? *Il a toujours été très correct envers toi.*'

'Please, Mummy; let's not start this thing all over again It was an accident.'

She sighed. 'I don't know why you are behaving so strangely all the time. I suppose you need a wife. I'll have to go and live with my sister when you are married.'

'Not at all,' I said. 'I'll never leave you. If I marry, you shall live with me.'

'Oh, that's what they all say. When you have a pretty wife all of your own, you won't want an old hag like myself hanging about.'

'You're not an old hag,' I said. 'You are still very attractive and I love you very much.'

'What do you want for lunch, dear?'

I wanted to smoke, but if I did that, it meant having to get up and go to the bathroom because that's the effect the first cigarette of the day has on me.

'Who do you think would marry me?' I asked.

'That won't be difficult,' she said. '*Après tout*, we still belong to one of the best families in Egypt.'

'Vicky Doss,' I said, 'would accept me, I hear.'

'She hasn't got a penny.'

'Neither have I.'

She sighed and continued with her work.

'Mummy?'

'What is it, dear?'

'Mummy, what do you think of Edna Salva?'

She didn't answer.

'Well?'

'You might as well know, people say she took you to London as her gigolo.'

'It's not true,' I said.

'I know. *Mais les gens parlent, tu sais.*'

'Would you like me to marry her?'

She put the socks down and said she didn't care whom I married as long as she knew I was happy. She knew, she said, that Edna had been my girl friend. But, she said, marrying a Jewess '*ce n'est pas très pratique en ce moment*', but if I loved her and if that was the reason why I was behaving the way I did, I might as well marry her. If she would accept me, that is; because they were multi-millionaires. She was also older than me, my mother said. Suddenly she told me to marry for love and started weeping.

The telephone rang. My mother took her glasses off and her usual look returned.

'*C'est* Dr Hamza,' she whispered. 'Be very polite.' She brought me the telephone and stood expectantly by.

'Ram,' he shouted.

'Yes?'

'What have you done with the last set of pictures?'

'I have,' I said, 'made copies and sent them to all the newspaper editors.'

'Who gave you permission to do such a thing?'

'Nobody,' I said.

'You are an irresponsible child,' he shouted. 'You are not only endangering yourself, but everyone else connected with this business. Burn everything you have. Don't come to my office any more.' He hung up.

'What does he want?' my mother asked.

'Nothing,' I said.

'I heard what he said, Ram. You are connected with politics. I knew it,' she screamed. '*C'est la fin.* You will kill us all. *Mon dieu. Mon dieu . . .*'

I calmed her down, then went into the bathroom. I lay on the floor and reached with my hand under the bath-tub.

I reached for a loose tile and pulled from underneath it a large brown envelope. I placed it in the sink and set light to it. I replaced the tile, cleaned everything, then started dressing.

PART V

I knocked at Edna's door. Once, in London, when we had been particularly close, she had said that if we were to part for ever, she would cut her hair because she could not bear to know that I would not comb it for her any more. I too, I had said, could not bear to think that anyone else would comb her hair.

'Come in, Ram.' She recognized my knock. She was sitting at her desk writing a letter, a cigarette in her hand and a cup of Turkish coffee beside her paper. She was going to get up but I told her to go on writing. I pulled a chair and sat behind her.

'Writing a letter?' I asked.

'Yes.'

'Do you have a large family, Edna?'

'I am my parents' only child, you know that. But the family is very large.'

'Where are they all living?'

'All over the world, Ram. All the Salvas of Germany and the Baltic countries are now mostly in South Africa, Rhodesia . . . around there. Then I have cousins and aunts in England, France, North America. All over the world, Ram.'

'And in Israel too?'

She shook her head. 'Some young ones from France and England are there. But more as tourists than anything else.'

'Are they all so very rich?'

'There are Salva shops all over the world. You know how we Jews are. We like to employ Jews, and better still, those belonging to the family. We also help each other a tremendous amount.'

'Edna, why are you living in this quarter?'

'Our house is *séquestré,* Ram, as well as our shops here. I like the district and I haven't made plans for the future yet.'

'What are your plans, Edna?'

She didn't answer.

'Edna, don't you want to get married and have children of your own and have them jump up on your knees and look at you with large eyes and ask you if they may have another ice?'

She smiled.

'And to have a husband who will place the children in convenient places on the floor; fix the automatic camera and rush back to put his hand on your shoulder for the family portrait?'

'You're sweet, Ram.'

'And then,' I said, 'when the camera has clicked, it is one of those new things which develop and print the film all at once, you will see that I have made a grimace and we shall both . . .'

'You, Ram?'

'Yes, me.' I looked at the nape of her neck. Her two plaits had been rolled up and stuck on either side of her head, covering her ears. Her neck is slender and pale, with a concave line running down the middle of her nape, like a girl of twelve.

'It will never be, Ram.'

'If you only gave me a reason,' I said. 'There are hundreds. One would do. Or just say you don't love me.'

'I do love you,' she whispered.

I put my hands on the back of the chair and stared at her in silence. 'When you went away from London that first time and didn't write for a year, I used to walk the streets at night, wondering what happiness and the fulfilment of life really is. Perhaps it is only my personal opinion, perhaps it is because you have engendered that feeling in me; but happiness, to me, is the freedom of two people who love each other to share their lives in circumstances permitting this love to live. When I hear of downtrodden people, of concentration camps, of wars, of hunger, of imprisonment, I always think of two people separated in these circumstances. I know that people can't continue to love if they have to share a room with their children, or are diseased or are dirty or are hungry. In spite of your idealism, generosity, kindness, I consider you cruel. You are cruel when you say you love me, and yet insist on living separated from me. If you didn't love me, it would be another . . .'

'Please, Ram. Stop it.'

'Is there nothing, nothing at all I can do?'

She shook her head.

A man can sometimes run a marathon race over a fantastic distance, and when the race is ended, he collapses, exhausted, just as though he had measured his capacity to that very last inch.

I stretched my hand and touched her rolled plait. Suddenly I jumped up and stood with my hand outstretched, as though terribly stung. The plait fell from my hand to the floor, unrolling itself and looking at me desperately. She had cut her hair.

I had reached that last inch.

I was sitting on her bed, and she was by my side, holding my hand. The reason why she would never discuss marriage, was because she was already married. It was like asking the marathon racer, the collapsing marathon racer, to race again.

'I am already married, Ram,' she had said.

'To whom?' I asked, half an hour later.

'I married just before I met you. He was a Jew, a member of the Communist Party here. A very good man, Ram. Very honest, very kind. Utterly unselfish. We knew he was going to be arrested, and as I had a British passport, we hoped that if he married me, they would not imprison him. The British refused to give him asylum or nationality. He refused to go to the Soviets because they were supporting Nasser. He was suddenly completely alone. Two weeks after we were married, he was taken away and given ten years. A group of them tried to escape, and some of them died, shot with Russian weapons given to Nasser. He was hit by three bullets and is completely disfigured. He is not even a man any more. He is in Israel because he is a Jew.'

'It doesn't matter,' I said.

'I wanted so many times to tell you.'

'It doesn't matter,' I repeated.

'But I didn't. When I left you and went to Israel, I did not mean to come back . . . but I wanted so much to see you again. I am also a woman, Ram. Also weak like other women. I love too, like other women. Forgive me, Ram.'

'I forgive you a thousand times over,' I said.

I walked about the room, opening her cupboard and closing it; pulling her drawers out and pushing them in again.

'Are you becoming an alcoholic, Ram?'

I shook my head. She opened her desk and gave me an un-opened bottle of whisky.

'Will you have a glass too?'

'Yes.'

I opened the bottle and poured two glasses.

'So you are an Israeli,' I said.

'No, Ram, I am Egyptian.'

I stood up. 'You know, Edna, you are not Egyptian. Not because you are married to an Israeli or because you are Jewish; you are just not Egyptian. I'll tell you why. Do you remember you told me once that I am not Egyptian because I belong to the *élite*, etc? But I am Egyptian. Like Jameel and Yehia, I am real Egyptian. I have our humour. Even though my "Egyptian" has been enfeebled by my stay in England and by the books I have read, I have the Egyptian character. You haven't,' I told her. 'You have no humour, Edna. We would all have died a long time ago if we didn't have our humour.'

'I haven't got much to laugh about,' she said.

'God,' I said, going to her. 'I loved you and love you more than anything in the world, and these last six years would have been the happiest ever lived, if you had had some humour and not frowned upon mine; if you could have been light-hearted at times. It wouldn't have made any difference if you were married or not. It still doesn't make any difference. Do I care? We can live together until we die and that's all I care about. You know I can get a job any time I want. My aunt would see to that. Or we could go and live in Upper Egypt with my uncle. Even open a school there, if you wanted.'

I drank another glass of whisky.

'If it's politics,' I said bitterly, 'that I lack, I'll find something to do.' I told her about Dr Hamza.

'Why didn't you tell me about that before?'

'Did you ever give me a chance? You always refused to see me since my return. There are many things you don't know.'

'What, Ram?'

'I joined the Communist Party when I was in England.'

'You! Why?'

'Why? Oh, it would be easy to say I joined for the same reason anybody else joins – a belief in its principles.'

'Is that why you joined?'

I started walking round the room again. I finished my whisky and poured another glass. I don't like whisky very much without soda and ice, but I drank it all the same.

'I joined,' I said, 'because I didn't know what to do with the knowledge I possess.'

'What do you mean, Ram?'

'I mean,' I said, 'this knowledge of history and politics and literature had to be channelled towards something or other if I weren't to go mad. At first all I did – my politics, my behaviour, my infidelities – were nothing but bravado, showing off, enjoyment. I would go with you and listen to speeches about South Africa, go to rallies in Trafalgar Square, listen to Bevan and Russell and Soper and Collins and Paul Robeson singing; and then walk back home holding your hand, telling myself: what an interesting and enjoyable life this is. I would feel passionately angry about the cruelty and injustices I heard about, but this passionate anger was itself enjoyable. It was the participation with you in something good which I enjoyed. I loved you and that was the main thing in my life. It was when you would suddenly leave and I imagined I had lost you for good, that my anger at things political became personal. My bitterness at losing you became mingled with the atrocities I heard and read about. It was as though I had lost you because of people likeVerwoerd. And even when I was honest enough to admit that your leaving me had nothing to do with the injustices of the world, I would nevertheless believe that if the world had been just, we would have loved and lived normally, you and I.

'Edna,' I went on, 'when you used to leave, I used to be left with a colossal amount of knowledge and awareness of the world which I didn't know what to do with. As long as you were with me, it had, however vaguely, something to do with my love for you. My knowledge made me a little worthy of you.'

I filled our glasses once more.

'I left you that first time without writing,' Edna said, 'because I was afraid. You changed so quickly during that brief spell in England, I thought perhaps it was because of my influence on you. To prove to me, perhaps, that you were a man. I didn't want that. There was another reason why I left. But I could have written.' She finished her glass in one gulp and re-filled it herself.

She looked at me.

'Ram, I fell in love with you twice. The first time was because I was lonely and because you had a beautiful character. You were fresh and sincere. I am older than you, Ram. I thought your love for me would die naturally after a while. When I returned to England a year later, you had changed completely. You had become a difficult and complicated person. I fell in love with you again. But it was another love.

I loved you because I found you attractive . . . you are attractive to women. Give me a light, Ram.'

I lit her cigarette.

'Why,' I asked softly, 'do you say you loved me, when you always acted as though you didn't?'

She made a dismissing gesture with her hand. 'Because we can't get married. And even if we could, you would never be happy with me.'

'Why do you say that?'

'I knew it for certain when Didi came to England.'

'It is one of those circles you find no beginning to,' I said. 'I can say that what happened between Didi and myself was because I felt you didn't love me, and you can say you felt we couldn't be happy because of this business with Didi.'

'Ram, darling . . .' I suddenly smiled.

'I wonder why,' I said, 'we never used terms of endearments between us. Things like "darling" and "beloved". This is the first time you call me "darling".'

'Yes,' she said, 'it's true, we never did. I don't know why.' She shrugged her shoulders in a light, pleasant way and also smiled.

'I was going to tell you, Ram, that when Didi was in England, your old natural character returned for a while.'

I also shrugged my shoulders.

'When did you join the Communist Party?' she asked.

'I joined the last time you left, you and Font; just before the Suez war.'

'What really made you join?'

I filled my glass with whisky once more and stood looking out of the window. Heat has always had the strange effect of making a din in my ears; a perpetual low buzz I become aware of now and then, like suddenly hearing a clock's tick. I shook my head involuntarily.

'If,' I told Edna, 'someone has read an enormous amount of literature, and has a thorough knowledge of contemporary history, from the beginning of this century to the present day, and he has an imagination, and he is intelligent, and he is just, and he is kind, and he cares about other people of all races, and he has enough time to think, and he is honest and sincere, there are two things can happen to him; he can join the Communist Party and then leave it, wallowing in its short-comings, or he can become mad. Or,' I said, 'if he is unconsciously insincere, he may join one of the many left-wing societies in Europe, and enjoy himself.'

I put my glass down on her desk and started walking about the room.

'And what are you, Ram?'

'I am insincere,' I said, 'but honest.'

'Are you still a communist?'

'A communist,' I said. 'A communist. You should ask me whether I belong to the Communist Party. The answer to which is no.'

'Why didn't you return with us during the Suez war? Why did you become so sarcastic? Why didn't you tell us you had joined the Communist Party?'

'Because,' I said, 'Font would have joined it too if he had known. But Font is sincere. He'd have gone on being an active communist here and he would have been imprisoned and tortured. And anyway I joined after you had left.'

'And now?'

'Now what?'

'What are you going to do?'

I walked about once more, drinking more whisky and beginning to feel its effect.

'You asked me,' I said, 'why I was so sarcastic and all that. You were the one always to remind me I'm Egyptian, and yet you never wanted me to behave the way Egyptians do. As long as . . .'

'Why did you return, Ram?'

I lit another cigarette and stood by the window once more.

'You told me so many times you love Egyptians. I, too, Edna, but unconsciously, not like you. Egypt to me is so many different things. Playing snooker with Doromian and Varenian the Armenians, is Egypt to me. Sarcastic remarks are Egypt to me – not only the fellah and his plight. Riding the tram is Egypt. Do you know my friend Fawzi? He can never give an answer that isn't witty . . . and yet he isn't renowned for it. He's an ordinary Egyptian. Last week I was riding the tram with him when a man stepped on his foot. "Excuse me," said the man, "for stepping on your foot." – "Not at all," said Fawzi, "I've been stepping on it myself for the last twenty-seven years" . . . How can I explain to you that Egypt to me is something unconscious, is nothing particularly political, or . . . or . . . oh, never mind,' I said.

'But why then aren't you living an ordinary life? Why aren't you working, why are you annoying your family, why did you help Dr Hamza?'

And once again this terrible feeling of oppression and this longing to explode everything and expire with the explosion came over me.

I put my face in my hands.

'This terrible knowledge I possess,' I said. 'All the literature I have read. You. This awareness of myself,' I told her, 'which started to afflict me as soon as I set foot in Europe. I see myself not only through Egyptian eyes, but through eyes which embrace the whole world in their gaze.'

'I can't understand all you say, Ram.' She came towards me and did something she had never done before. She knelt and looked up to me with tears in her eyes.

'My God,' she said, 'I never realized I had made you so lonely.'

We have no twilight in Egypt; but we have a large sun setting on the horizon, and a mauve light, more substance than colour, regretfully reaching out from all objects. This only lasts a few minutes, but it is the sign of a fresh breeze on the way, and suddenly the streets become animated, and lethargy, you feel, has just been vanquished.

I stood in the street not knowing what to do with myself. Unless you are an alcoholic or something like that, it is horrible to start drinking in the early afternoon. You experience moments of exhilaration and others of depression and you keep on drinking until it is time to go to bed. I wanted to return to Edna but knew I should not. I'd have liked to take her dancing at the Semiramis roof and have supper overlooking the Nile. I counted my money slowly. I had over a hundred pounds. A street boy came and cleaned my shoes while I was standing. I gave him a pound and told him to keep it. I walked across the street to the Mirandi bar and ordered a whisky. Then I went in the telephone booth and dialled Mounir's number.

'*Buona sera, Anna, come sta?*'

'*Sto bene, grazie, Signor Ram, e tu?*'   A nice, kindly woman this Anna, *femme de ménage* to my aunt and before that to my grandparents. I asked her if the American signora was there.

'*La signora Carolina?*'

'*Sì, Anna.*' But she wasn't there. They had all gone out. I walked to the Metro cinema and stood a bit under the air-conditioned entrance, looking at an American film star killing Korean proletarians in pictures. Then I walked to another cinema and saw the same film star with a stethoscope stuck to his ear. I went to the Egyptian museum, but was told it was closed. I sometimes like to go in and touch all the colossal things there. As I wasn't far from the Semiramis I went there and had another whisky in the downstairs bar. I nodded to Pietro the pianist and had a whisky sent over to him. Pietro played *I Kiss your Hand, Madame*, a song I once told him I liked. I went upstairs to the roof but it was too early, although the band was already there, also drinking whisky at the bar.

'*Tu viens ce soir, Ram?*' the band leader asked.

I went downstairs and out. I stood watching the feluccas sail by. After a while I started walking along the Nile's bank towards Garden City. Many of my friends live there. I passed Nackla Pasha's house. There were many cars parked there, including those of Assam the Turk and Jameel, which meant they were having a game. So I walked up the drive and rang the bell. Didi Nackla opened the door and pretended she wasn't surprised to see me. It was as though our time in London had never existed, or we had been together the day before. She's very poised and beautiful, Didi Nackla; she has eyes stretched a little at the ends like a Chinese and is a Doctor of Literature from the Sorbonne. Font used to be very much in love with her when he was fifteen. She works on a newspaper now.

'*Tu vas jouer?*' she asked.

'No,' I said. 'I don't gamble any more.'

'*Chic,*' she said, 'you are paying us a social visit.'

Levy is teaching her brother, dim-wit Hamo, Arabic and he is very much in love with her. He has never told me, but I know.

'Yes,' I said. Didi Nackla is one of those strange flowers which can suddenly blossom from a bed of weeds.

'Delighted,' she said, and curtsied jokingly.

'I'll visit your mother first,' I said, 'then come to you if I may.'

'Good,' she said. She has two rooms and a kitchen of her own in a wing of the house. Mrs Nackla, her mother, is blind, and it is the custom to stay with her a few minutes when visiting the house. A maid servant sitting at her feet told her who I was as I came in.

I kissed Mrs Nackla on both cheeks and sat on a chair facing her.

'How is your mother, Ram?'

'She is very well, thank you,' I said.

'And your aunt?'

'Which one?'

'Aida.'

'My Aunt Aida is very well, thank you,' I said.

'And your other aunt?'

'Which one?'

'Noumi.'

'My Aunt Noumi is very well, thank you,' I said.

'And how is your Aunt Samiha?'

'My Aunt Samiha,' I said slowly, 'is also very well, thank you.'

'I am glad to hear it.'

'My uncle in Upper Egypt is also well,' I said.

'I haven't asked,' she said.

'No, but you were going to.'

She laughed. She likes to laugh, Mrs Nackla, and also to hear the latest events and gossip. So I made myself comfortable and started.

'Marie,' I said, 'bought a new car for six thousand pounds because the old one was costing too much in petrol. Ti and Sina are in New York for their trousseau. My cousin Madi is engaged and will get married next month. Lolo is having an affair with a German industrialist and her husband is as impotent as ever.'

'You're a dog, Ram.'

'Well, it's the truth. Hassan Abdu, the eldest son of the Abdus, is getting married to a Norwegian girl. Lotfy Safwat, the husband of Gida, has been put in a concentration camp for being a communist. We shall never see *him* again. Claro Hanno has lost her jewels gambling in Italy. Farah Farah is divorcing his wife and marrying Fatma, the bellydancer. Kicko Rassoom is turning Moslem for business reasons. Assam the Turk, Yehia and Jameel are gambling with your husband in the next room. There is talk of a match between my cousin Mounir and your daughter Didi. I pushed the same Mounir in the swimming pool yesterday and now I am going to go and visit your daughter.'

'No, no, Ram, stay a bit. I want to laugh.' She nudged her maid with her foot. 'Go and call Jameel,' she said, 'I haven't had a good laugh for weeks.'

I lit a cigarette and waited. Jameel appeared in the doorway and ran towards me.

'Ram, Ram; some skin. Give me some skin; I haven't had a card the whole day long.'

'I can't,' I said, 'I've used all I have today.'

'Not a card, Mrs Nackla,' he moaned. 'I haven't had a winning hand the whole day long.'

'Give him some skin,' Mrs Nackla said.

'All right,' I said, 'I've still got a little bit left, but it's on my feet.'

'Give it to me,' Jameel said.

'But you know, skin from the feet must be picked by the mouth.'

'This is a well-known fact,' Mrs Nackla said. 'This morning my husband tried to pick some skin from my feet which I have been saving for my son Hamo's big game tomorrow. I thought it was the dog licking my feet.'

'You can laugh,' Jameel said. 'Assam the Turk swears he buys skin from a local skin-giver, and he's winning like anything.'

So I took my shoes and stockings off, and Jameel rubbed his mouth against my soles for luck while the maid translated the scene to Mrs Nackla. He rushed back to the gambling.

'This gambling,' Mrs Nackla complained; 'it's terrible. Now that they have closed the baccarat establishments, my husband grabs every visitor I have for a game. What happened to Font?' she suddenly asked.

'Nothing,' I said.

'Come, come, Ram. I've known him long enough. What is this foolishness of working like an ordinary . . .'

'He's gone mad,' I said, depressed now and annoyed.

'But . . .'

I left her and crossed two beautifully furnished halls to Didi's apartment. She was sitting, her legs pulled up beneath her, with a semicircle of skirt covering them; a delicate hand-made lamp-shade behind her sofa shed a soft light on the work in her hand; a book, leather, and instruments for book-binding. The walls of her sitting-room are lined with books she has read and then bound in leather herself. 'I have never bound a book I didn't like,' she once told me. The perimeter of the room with its mahogany and books, together with a large desk in a corner, would have given the room too masculine an appearance if it were not for a little circle of femininity in the corner she now occupied. A white, wrought-iron table with a light pink table-cloth, on which is set a blue tea-service for two. This corner is carpeted in plain brown and the sofa and single armchair are also upholstered in brown, but paler and of a shiny material, like satin.

'Sit down, Ram.'

'In a moment.' I walked around the room while she continued with her work. There was peace in that room, a peace which someone of my type hardly ever comes across or even knows of. Serenity: a serenity which suddenly descended upon me in its profound beauty. It had affected me before, but I didn't want to remember that now. The last time I had seen Didi was in London. I stood where she could not see me and watched her. Like Edna, she has no mannerisms or affected poses, except that her French education has given her a touch of coquetry which Edna lacks. She wore white sandals – a simple platform for her feet, with a single golden loop for her toe. Once, in London, we were lying on the grass in Hyde Park and I suddenly kissed her feet when Edna wasn't looking. On her desk is a tall, slender vase made of metal with an equally slender young rose shooting out of it, and near the vase a massive black candle on an iron stand. I lit the candle and walked a few steps away to watch the effect. The lunch-time and early afternoon whisky was beginning to tell. Headachey drowsiness and sudden heart palpitations. The unfilled moments of exhilaration, the frustration and depression. I could still see the serenity around me, but had already lost the power to feel it.

I sat down.

When Didi Nackla smiles, two tiny dots, dimples, suddenly appear on either side of her mouth and you are surprised because her face is perfectly smooth, without any lines to indicate the position of those dimples. She touched her necklace, a Nefertiti one made of brass and corals, then her hand went higher and touched her throat and neck. She smiled. 'If I hadn't chanced to open the door,' she said, 'you would be playing baccarat with my father and your friends.'

'Yes,' I said.

'Come into some money?'

'Played bridge with my cousin Mounir, then snooker with Doromian, the Armenian.'

'How long have you been back?'

'About a year.' I lit a cigarette then put it out quickly – nausea, and I wanted to vomit.

She continued with her book-binding. I stood up again, trying to fight the headache. When she was in London, I used to make her laugh. I used to describe the people living there and mimic them. I used to describe Paddy and speak like him. This business of love. And then Edna has no sense of humour. I used to mix politics and humour and love with Didi Nackla; but with Edna politics is politics. As it should be, I suppose.

I sighed.

This whisky. The headache had arrived in full force. I went into the bathroom, found aspirin, gargled, brushed my teeth with her tooth-brush, and started sucking a peppermint tablet.

'What happened after I left London?'

'I quarrelled with Font and Edna something terrible. The Suez war. I refused to return.' I sat down, then stood up, and kept moving about the room. I blew out the candle, then relit it. Then I sat down on her desk and started playing with a paper knife.

'I wrote you a long letter once,' I told her.

'I still have it.'

'Levy is in love with you,' I told her.

She didn't answer.

I went and sat on the arm of her sofa.

'And Font used to love you when he was fifteen; and I love you.' My temples were throbbing with pain.

'And Edna?'

'Yes, and Edna too.' I kicked the wire connection and her lamp went out. I caught the book in her hand and threw it on the floor, then lay on the sofa and put my head on her lap.

'Didi.'

'What is it?'

'Didi,' I said, 'Edna has been whipped in the face by an officer.' Her hand came down and gently pressed my head to her lap.

After a while she asked whether whisky or a cup of tea would do me any good.

Tea.

I woke up about midnight. The candle was still burning, a violin concerto was just audible, coming from the radio; my shoes were off and I was covered with a light blanket. I had no headache whatsoever and remained still, listening to the music.

'Are you awake?'

'Yes,' I said.

'I'll make some fresh tea.'

I put the lights on and pulled my knees up to my chin, still covered with the blanket.

'Tell me about Paddy,' she said from the kitchen. I could see her making sandwiches, opening and closing her fridge, humming bits of the concerto. She is happy. Everyone should be like Didi Nackla. I mean the world should be put in order and everyone should have a nice flat like Didi Nackla and go about humming tunes. Like birds.

'I lived there for a while, you know.'

'What did you say?'

'I lived in Vincent's house when Edna and Font returned to Egypt. Paddy and I used to sleep in the kitchen. He'd always be reading the Greyhound something or other.' I imitated Paddy's Irish brogue. 'Be Jeez, now,' he would say. 'I tell yer now, that dog can't be beaten.' He'd shake his head. 'Well, by God, that dog'll be half a mile in front of the others. Twenty to one at least. I wouldn't be surprised now, if Frank Maloney is in on this. Shirley,' he'd shout, 'd'yer know where your mother is, now?'

'No,' she'd shout back.

'I bet yer she's at the Whoite City now,' he'd tell me. 'Wouldn't say she was going. Be Jeez now, if that dog wins she'll be sorry now.'

'What's the dog's name?' I'd ask Paddy.

'Trafalgar the Third,' he'd say. 'A foine dog, I tell yer. Well I tell yer now I saw his gran'father, t'was in Cork and this Frank Maloney comes to me and says: Paddy, he says, if you can raise the price of two tickets so we can travel with that dog to the Whoite City, we're alroit, boy. He had twenty pound he showed me; that was to put on the dog, now. Well, I tell yer I ran home as fast as me legs would go. The old man was out havin' a drink and I go up to his room and under the mattress, be Jeez, a bunch of five-pound notes wrapped up in an old towel.' He'd stop talking and laugh. 'Well I tell yer, no sooner am I with Frank Maloney, than I see me father come as fast as he could towards us. He was an old man but, be Jeez, he could run fast. Well there we were; me and Maloney running as fast as we could towards the station, and Pa running behind us brandishin' his stick. Well I tell yer, if that train started half a second later, he would have caught us, now.'

So I'd ask Paddy if the dog won.

'Well I tell yer truthfully now. I swear that dog was the best Whoite City ever saw.'

Shirley would come in and stand near the door. 'He was the best dog there,' she'd tell me, 'but all the other dogs were doped except Trafalgar the First, so naturally he

200

arrived a mile behind the others; and Paddy didn't dare go back to his father for a couple of years.'

'Be Jeez,' Paddy would say, 'The old man had a nasty temper I can tell yer. Well I remember now going to Dublin with him and a man called Jimmy O'Donovan . . .'

Didi was laughing.

'How long did you live there?' she asked.

'About a year. This Paddy was terribly lazy and would keep sitting for weeks on end doing nothing. Sometimes his friends would come with cases of Guinness: "An how are yer, Paddy Tynan? I bet me wages, Paddy Tynan, you have two large callus on the seat of your trousers. Let's have a peep, Paddy Tynan. You'll be walkin' on your backside soon, be Jeez". '

'Were you content, living there?'

'You know, Didi, this reading too much, and Font and Edna being away, used to make me feel very lonely at times.'

'Why did you leave?'

'The police found me. I hit a policeman in Trafalgar Square during the Suez war and my visa had expired and not been renewed. Besides which it was impossible for me to work anywhere and I had no money. It is funny how all my *New Statesmen* friends and fellow "intellectuals" dropped me one by one when I was in trouble. All except Vincent. Even the Dungates, you know. Anyway, I was thrown out of England.'

'What did you do then?'

'Went to Germany because it was the only place I could go without a visa. I worked in factories here and there. But never mind all that now.'

'Why did you come back?'

'Probably because of Font. I kept on seeing his eyebrows going higher and higher in amazement at this world around him and then . . .'

'Then what?'

'I like Font very much, you know. And then, Didi,' I said, 'I thought I could do something useful. Teach or something like that; even help in villages and things. You know, Didi Nackla, I am . . .' I was going to tell her I wasn't as bad as I seemed, but didn't.

'Even with you, Didi. I mean I told you frankly I loved Edna. Do you remember how we laughed? With Edna I was never really natural, I don't know why. Anyway, when I came back I saw that life here is exactly as it used to be. Even to the Mahrousa. I mean how can I go and work in a boiling village when *he* is travelling about in Farouk's yacht which costs a million just for upkeep? And all this nationalization business makes me laugh, although I don't tell Font that. The money goes to that useless army. Even the Asswan dam; by the time it's completed we'll have increased by ten million.'

'What do you want him to do?'

'Birth control and all that.'

'He would become unpopular.'

'And Israel too. Imagine a third of our income being pumped into an army to fight a miserable two million Jews who were massacred something terrible in the last war. So what if he becomes unpopular? He is strong enough to take unpopular steps. Besides, you know, we Egyptians don't care one way or another about Israel. No, Didi Nackla,' I said, 'it's stupid living under a police state without the benefits of the control.'

'What do you mean?'

'Oh, don't be stupid. If we are to live under a dictatorship, it should be a communist one. I'll tell you what I mean. Look at India. The people are paying for having a democracy by starving. The Chinese are not starving at all and can look to the future with confidence, because they have a communist dictatorship. Whereas we have the worst of both systems. Both the dictatorship and the starving without any future to look forward to. Not,' I said, suddenly laughing, 'that there is much starving going on in *our* circles.'

'And what do Font and Edna think of all that?'

'I can't speak to them that way. They're full of theories and ideals and political sophistication, it makes me laugh. Font used to walk from Aldermaston to London, and Edna travels third-class in our trains as a mark of equality. A fat lot of good that will do.'

She poured me another cup of tea.

'It's nice sitting here talking to you,' I said. 'It's nice and cosy and comfortable and you are so beautiful.'

She smiled.

'I nearly broke my heart over you in England,' she said. 'You have a terrible charm.'

'Why didn't you?'

'Why didn't I what?'

'Break your heart.'

'You are intelligent enough to know I wouldn't take someone like you seriously.'

'Yes,' I said, 'I know,' and laughed.

'All this nonsense,' she said, 'the three of you.'

'Yes,' I said.

'The Spanish civil war,' she remembered our discussions and activities in London. She had lived eight months with us. 'The bomb, the British elections, the Independent Labour Party, Father Huddleston, the little theatre in the East End . . .'

'Yes,' I said.

'*Entre nous*,' she said, 'it suited you. You were very attractive, always elegantly dressed among the polo-necks and duffle coats. I liked the love part, too,' she said. 'It was a holiday I enjoyed. But it was a holiday and it ended.'

'*Cliché*,' I said.

'What is *cliché*?'

'A holiday and it ended.'

'It was also intolerable, *cette affaire*, for Edna. Don't think she didn't notice I often spent the night in your room. Why she put up with . . .'

'Do you know,' I said, 'when Edna suddenly left England the first time, I began to learn of the terrible pain of love. She did not write or say where she was for a whole year. And when she came back, all she said was that she had gone to Israel and lived for a year in a Kibbutz, she had a British passport in addition to her Egyptian one I discovered; as though that was enough reason to explain not writing for a year. Six months later she was off again, to South Africa this time. She put more money for us in the bank and was off again without telling me where. Just before you came I had asked her to marry me.'

'And?'

'And,' I said, 'the answer was no. Why then are we lovers? Why don't you put a stop to this? Because I love you, she says and looks sad.'

'Don't you love her any more?' Didi asked.

I didn't answer.

'Many people of your age like to revolt a little,' Didi said. 'Many Egyptians too. I find the régime here good.'

'What do you mean?' I said, my voice slightly raised.

She looked puzzled for a moment at my pitch.

'The government is good and fair. If some people like you and Font want to be a bit theatrical – you'll soon get over it.'

'Soon get over it? Do you know Bobby Malla? He's dead. Killed in a concentration camp. Do you know Hakima Mohammed who used to be with you at school and caused a scandal because she married a Copt? Her husband buried her mutilated body last week. She "committed suicide" they told him. Do you know the number of young men, doctors, engineers, lawyers in concentration camps? Or don't you know that we have concentration camps?' I shouted. I stood up. 'You bloody idiot,' I said, 'you can sit back and engrave your name on leather for your books while hundreds of decent young people are dying and being imprisoned and you call it "theatrical". You're a bitch like all the rest,' I shouted. 'You and your bloody education and *doctorat*. You're working for a muzzled press, aren't you? A bloody editor you are; just write what they tell you, don't you?'

'Ram! Are you mad to scream so?'

'Yes, I *am* mad. Did you or did you not know that "twelve men committed suicide" this week in concentration camps and the prison doctor, glory to him, refused to sign the death certificates? Did you or didn't you?' I screamed.

She didn't answer.

'Because I posted the pictures and the documents myself to you and all the other editors. Not a word appeared, you cowards and backside lickers, all of you!' I completely lost control of myself. I had seen the pictures of the distorted faces of the twelve. One of them I had known at the university. A quiet, peaceful boy from Upper Egypt, son of a fellah. He used to live on seven pounds a month he earned working as a cinema usher in the evenings. A scholarly Marxist who had refused to fight against Israel unless Nasser met Ben Gurion for an attempt at a peaceful solution. He went away quietly, his neighbours had told me, and was never heard of again until I saw that picture.

'Not so loud, Ram.'

I sat down. It had been so nice and peaceful, waking up and drinking tea with her.

'I'm sorry, Didi. I didn't mean to be so loud. I'll go home now.'

'No. The gardener closes the gate at night and I don't want him to see you leave my room so late.'

'Still, I'm sorry,' I said. 'Only a moment ago I was thinking everyone on earth should be like you.'

She stood up and ruffled my hair with her hand. 'You are a child, Ram. But I like you.' Then she sat on my lap and put one arm round my neck.

'Kiss me like you used to.'

She smiled and I kissed the dimples on either side of her cheeks.

'Nobody,' she whispered, 'has touched me since you did in London.' She had been a virgin.

'What is it, Ram?'

'Nothing.'

'You suddenly laughed.'

'I was dreaming.' She rubbed her cheek against my chest then covered my body with hers. I felt the weight of her, relaxed and cool. I passed my hands up and down from the nape of her neck to the small of her back.

'You are damp,' I told her.

'I've had a bath.'

'Why?'

'I wanted to be fresh and cool for you when you woke. Do you like my bedroom?'

'Yes,' I said.

'And me?'

'And you too,' I whispered. 'You are very beautiful.'

'Hold me tight and say beautiful things to me.' Her heart uttered quick little beats and her breasts stiffened against me.

There comes a moment, after that, when man's passion has suddenly been completely vented, and all that remains is a detached, aloof, perhaps rather smug omnipotence. And if the man is not really in love with the woman, she is at a terrible disadvantage. He has a sudden lingering ascendancy over someone who a little while ago was his equal.

Although Didi is very sophisticated and frequents sophisticated circles, this part of her life, this essence, has to be unfulfilled unless she is married. It was nearly by force I took her, that first time in London. Now she lay in bed, her serenity ruffled, and a naïve, helpless expression on her face.

'I am in love with you,' she said.

And this omnipotence a man feels usually makes him

cruel. Smug, as I said. And the crueller he is, the more helpless and defeated is his companion.

'First,' I said, 'you should never tell a man you love him in this way. It makes him cruel. Second, if you had the courage to give yourself to someone else, you would also fall in love with him.'

'No,' she said.

'My Aunt Noumi,' I told her, 'is arranging a match between you and my cousin Mounir.'

She shook her head.

I turned over and lay face downwards, putting my head under the pillow.

'Or,' I said, 'if you don't like Mounir, you might as well marry me.'

She ran her hand up and down my shoulders and back.

'Don't make fun of me, Ram.'

'I am very serious.' I turned round and faced her. 'Will you marry me?'

'But . . .'

'But what?'

'But . . . but . . .'

'But but but but,' I mimicked. 'If you love someone, you marry him.'

'But . . .'

'But,' I repeated.

'But . . .'

'But,' I said and laughed.

'But, Ram, you have no job, no money.'

'That's right; that's why you'll get married to Mounir.'

'Besides . . .'

'Besides nothing. Mounir has a set of books he bought in

America about love-making. I saw them; with figures and positions. One chapter is entitled ''The Perfect Five Minutes''. The designs are drawn on a background of a clock with a second's hand. For the first four minutes he ''arouses'' you, and for another full minute he benefits from his ''arousation'', if there is such a word. Besides, you can always shove a cushion in your place if you're not inclined. It will remind him of his days of training. He has shown me the books: ''You sure pick up some information there, boy.'' '

'And Edna,' Didi asked.

'I am finished with Edna,' I said.

'Besides . . .'

'What, another besides?'

'Be serious. How did you get all this literature and pictures of the concentration camps?'

'A hobby of mine,' I said.

'Through Font?'

'Font? *Font*. Can you see these things in Font's hand? He'd have rushed in the street and given a copy to everyone he saw; and before they even shot him, he'd have gone mad. No,' I said, 'leave Font in his snooker heaven out of harm's way.'

'Do you belong to the Communist Party?'

'There is no such thing, I tell you. Together with the liberals, social democrats, pacifists and idealists; they're on the shores of the Red Sea. We have a lot of Ex-SS Germans here who know what to do with such people.'

'Say the truth, Ram.'

'I tell you, it's only a hobby of mine. You know me better than to think I'd sacrifice my comfort or life for anything.'

'But you don't love me, Ram. Why did you want to marry me?'

I pulled her against me and kissed her. 'I shall love you,' I said. 'There were times in London I was madly in love with you. You are terribly beautiful. I want to live with you in a beautiful house with lots of books bound in leather. To take you out each evening to the poshest places. To go for drives in the desert in our car. To caress you and make love to you every night. To buy you the most beautiful clothes, jewels, perfumes in existence . . .' and I involuntarily laughed – this tic of mine of suddenly laughing – 'with your own money of course. Because you are very rich.'

'So you *are* joking.'

'No. I'd have been joking if I hadn't mentioned you are rich. You don't think I'd have asked you to marry me if you were poor? How could we have lived? Precisely because you are rich, I am serious.' I held her closer and when she began to speak again, I covered her mouth with mine. We lay in silence for a while, until I felt passion stirring within me again. 'I want you to endow our house with serenity,' I said. 'With serenity and peacefulness. To go about the house humming tunes, both of us.'

'I have always been in love with you,' she said.

'It's me Didi is marrying,' I told my mother, 'not Mounir.'

'*C'est le comble*,' my mother started. '*Ça c'est le comble . . .*'

'Didi and I are going to get married,' I repeated.

'You are joking. *Ce n'est pas possible.*'

'I am not joking'. I said. 'Unless you want me to give her up for Mounir.'

'I can't believe it.'

'It is true. We got engaged in London,' I lied.

'But what will your aunt say?'

'I'll tell you when I see her this afternoon.'

'Where?'

'Didi is going with them to Kirka. I am meeting them there.'

'But she has arranged everything.'

'What?'

'The new villa in Heliopolis for them, and Nackla Pasha was delighted . . .'

'What about Didi?' I asked.

'She gave no definite answer. I swear she never said she was engaged to you or to anyone else; all she said was that she would think about it . . . *et nous avons tous cru* . . .'

'Or don't you want your son to marry Didi?' I said. 'This charming person . . . this millionairess? Of course I shall not marry against your wishes.'

The situation was too much for her. She took her handkerchief out and started rubbing her eyes.

'Buy her an expensive present,' she said after a while. 'Let them send the bill here and not to your aunt.'

'La Edna' was anyhow much too old for me, she added.

This shop. You enter it and the croquet lawn at the club comes to mind. It's the sort of shop which has a mile-long window with nothing in it but a black beret and a rose.

Gaston was walking in the entrance hall with his hands behind his back. Gaston is *maître de cérémonie* in that shop. He is one of the people called Gaston but who are a bit Maltese, a bit Italian, some Greek and probably something East European. He came towards me.

'*Bonjour, bonjour, monsieur,*' he said. 'The family is upstairs. May I congratulate you on the engagement of your cousin?'

'You may,' I said. Gaston, as I said, is a mixture of many races, but he and his parents were born in Egypt. Yet he doesn't speak a word of Arabic. This shop is going to be 'nationalized'. I put nationalized in inverted commas because I don't think it has any economic significance here, except to enrich the army somewhat. But this business of nationalization will be significant as far as Gaston is concerned, because he will have to stop using about the only Arabic word he knows, which is 'go away', and which he has been allowed to use all his life to ninety-five per cent of the Egyptian population. I remember when the Suez Canal was nationalized and a lot of share-owners and blimps were furious. It is a very good thing this canal was nationalized, particularly to those who knew the French club in Port Fouad and saw the French having cushy jobs and being arrogant to everyone. (A British blimp is very often a figure of fun and his entourage of horsy young women and nasal, public-school nincompoops doesn't look so bad when you compare it to a crowd of French middle-class bourgeois.) This Suez Canal Company was a heaven for the very worst type of French string-pulling good-for-nothings. They sat in the club doing nothing all day long, and once Font and I parked a car in front of that club – a battered old car we had used for a Suez expedition, from which we had thrown some inefficient bombs at the British army camp. We stopped the car in front of that French club and went in for a drink of whisky.

'*Pssst . . . vous là-bas,*' a Frenchman shouted and pointed to the exit.

'*Allez vous faire foutre,*' Font said. We went to the bar and ordered a whisky.

'No,' said the barman. Suddenly about five Frenchmen popped up with sticks – they actually drove us out with sticks, big, fat, wooden sticks. But that was not all. While we were having a fight outside on the balcony, another group of Frenchmen bodily removed our small Fiat and threw it on the beach. When the police came, it was *us* they took away. I tell you, when that canal was nationalized, Font and I could have kissed the Colonel's feet in admiration.

But back to the shop. Gaston led me to the lift and spared me climbing about eight steps. This shop. People go to it as a sort of *apéritif*; I mean they don't go there to *buy* anything, or because they need something or other: no. They have a coffee with the director, and they talk about Paris and Rome and New York, and then they remember Budapest in the old days and wonder what happened to La Comtesse Ozbensky . . . what a delightful creature, that Nina! And Luigi, the director, tells them '*c'était une reine . . .*' and they all shake their heads sadly: what *is* happening in the world, they ask. Finally they remember that even with them things are not quite the same. It's increasingly difficult to travel, Luigi, and even then, with all the worry about making arrangements for adequate money to be waiting for them there . . . it's not only Budapest and Prague, *mon cher*, and they all nod knowingly. Then Sousou tells them about Tata who is very '*débrouillarde, ma chère*', and officially sends seventy pounds a month to an imaginary student-son in Switzerland . . . with this she has enough money for a few weeks in Lausanne each year. Luigi laughs at this, then puts his finger in front of his mouth and tells them to be careful . . . one never knows. Finally he suddenly remembers something. 'Have I told you?' he asks. 'I have four new Diors I haven't yet opened.' – '*Pas possible!* Do show us, Luigi, *ne sois pas méchant.*' 'Yes, yes,' he tells them; 'but not today.' '*Ouf, Luigi, ne sois pas antipathique* . . . we're only going to have a look at them.' Then they fight over the dresses amongst themselves; and when Luigi shows them the new shoes he has received from Italy, they furnish their entire family with shoes from Italy to last them five years. An hour or so later, Luigi is giving orders to pack the three or four thousand pounds' worth of stuff he has just sold. Then he rings up Madame Abdulla – better known as Fifi. 'Have I told you,' he says, 'about the things I have just received from Vienna?'

I went out of the lift and stood with my hand in my pocket. I looked round and then saw my aunt. She was holding court.

I know this court business well. Now and then she has all the family to spend the day at her villa. All of us, rich, poor, and genuinely poor; priests, clerks, poor girls saving for their dowry, second and third cousins, great aunts and uncles.

'Now, Samia,' she will start, 'I want you to get married to Fathy. Do you hear, Fathy?'

'Yes, my aunt.'

'Next month or so. I don't want any more nonsense now. Age makes no difference. He has a good job and that's all that matters.' This Fathy would be about twenty-five years older than the miserable girl.

'Yes, my aunt.' Then she will give Samia a dozen of Mounir's silk shirts and tell her to embroider Mounir's initials as recompense for having forced her to marry repulsive-looking Fathy.

'Yes, my aunt . . . thank you my aunt, thank you.'

'Aziz, you are to stick to that job you have. If I hear once more that you arrive late or smell of alcohol, you shall never enter this house again. Do you hear?'

'Yes, my aunt.'

'Now look here, Amin. The church is in a filthy state, you must increase the price of the Holy Bread; I am not a one-woman charitable organization to pay for everything. If you don't increase the price of the bread, I shall talk to the Patriarch. That's final. Another thing; place two or three ten-piastres notes in the offering-plate before passing it round.'

'Yes, my aunt.'

Having settled the affairs of these, she will start moving up the scale until she reaches my mother and speaks in French.

'You must sell your car, Vivi.'

'I shall see,' my mother will say.

Now she was filling a large sofa. My girl-cousin Mado was getting married and my aunt was there to see she bought the right things.

'Nonsense,' her squeaky voice jetted, 'you'll throw it away at the end of a week. Show me that *crêpe-de-Chine* again, Luigi.' He hurried away. 'No, no. I've said no, and Mado it *means* no.' My cousin Mado is as rich as my aunt, but has no courage.

My aunt's eyes are large, protruding globes, hanging, it seems, from underneath her eybrows. I saw them flash me a glance, sideways, a fraction of a second, then back again to the cloth Marie was holding in front of her.

I shook myself and sat about ten yards away from them. Luigi nodded to me and I nodded back. I heard him order a young man to bring me a coffee. Didi Nackla sat on a sofa opposite that of my aunt, with Mounir by her side. She glanced at me now and then. My coffee came, and was placed on an antique table by my side. I lit a cigarette. I was thinking about Edna's husband and idly wondering what he looked like, when the people around my aunt dispersed a bit. She was getting up. First a hand on a servile shoulder, then up, and a little bend on one side, pulling that side of her corset down. Then another bend on the other side, pulling that side of her corset down; then a quick grimace, and she was ready to walk. She wobbled up to me, searched in her handbag for a handkerchief, blew her nose, and calmly sat next to me.

'Give me one of your Egyptian cigarettes,' she said, 'Mounir's Americans are too strong for me.'

I gave her a cigarette and lit it for her. She waved her hand in a 'go away' sign to some cousins and others who were edging towards us to hear the conversation.

'What is this I hear about you and Didi Nackla?'

'We are going to get married,' I said.

'So, so,' she mused.

'So, so,' I repeated.

'There is no point in being either rude or arrogant.'

'I am sorry,' I said, depressed and miserable.

'And how are you going to support your wife?'

'She is rich enough,' I said.

'Aha. It is the money that is attracting you?'

'Money is attractive,' I said.

'Aha . . .'

I put my cigarette out and folded my arms.

'And your mother?'

'What about my mother?'

'How is she going to live?'

'What do you mean,' I asked.

'Your father lost all he had on the *bourse* and I am supporting your mother – not to mention you. There is no question of me giving her a penny if Didi does not marry Mounir.'

'Didi has enough money.'

'And did you tell Didi that?'

'I shall,' I sighed.

'Aha.' She took her handkerchief out once more and blew her nose.

'How far did you get with your studies here and in England?'

'Why do you ask?'

'Just answer me.'

'Oh, I can get a degree any time I want.'

'So, so.'

'Yes,' I said.

'It is your last chance, Ram. I shall never repeat this offer. You can go to Cook's or some other travel agency and book a ticket on a plane or a ship to London, or anywhere else you want. I shall pay for yet another four years of studies. You will get an adequate monthly allowance; you can also buy a small car. So there. Don't stretch my patience and generosity too far.'

'Thank you,' I said. 'But I shall marry Didi Nackla all the same.'

'So, so.'

'So, so,' I repeated.

She nodded to Mounir and he came towards us, his hand outstretched.

'Sure needed some drying out, cousin,' he said, shaking hands. 'But I guess I got no hard feelings.'

'Thank you,' I said. 'It was an accident.'

'We sure did drink quite a bit, eh?'

'Yes,' I said.

'Boy, it's great having two beautiful women at home. I guess there is something doing there, buddy.'

'Perhaps,' I said.

'C was asking about you. Sure made a hit, there.'

'Who's C,' I asked.

'Caroline.'

'I see.'

'Hey, Ram. How about you going to the States for a while, eh?'

'No thanks, Mounir.'

'You don't wanna worry about anything. I've got it all here.' He tapped his wallet-pocket.

'Thanks.'

'Look, I wanna talk to you, man to man, eh?'

'All right,' I said. We left his mother and went to another sofa.

'I guess I'm pretty keen on Didi, and boy, it sure came as a surprise about you and her. Well, I said to myself; that guy Ram's had a hard deal; his pop losing that cash on the *bourse*. Well, I said to myself, what would you have done in his place, Mounir? And d'you know, boy? I'd have done exactly like you.' He tapped me on the shoulder. 'You gotta have a standard of living, boy; a car, money, get

218

around. Didi's A1, eh? Boy, look at those curves.' He winked. 'Well, I gotta proposition right here . . .'

'Mounir,' I said. 'Didi Nackla is sitting there. If she wants to marry you, she marries you; if she wants to marry me, she marries me. That's all there is to it.'

'I've sure been talking to her.'

'What did she say?'

'Well . . .'

'Did you tell her I was marrying her for her money?'

'I guess I did, cousin.'

'And what did she say?'

'I guess she gave no answer.'

'Well,' I said. 'I shall go and talk to her myself.'

She was sitting alone in a corner.

'Didi, I'm fed up with all this. You know they're trying to bribe me. I've told you before I wouldn't have asked you to marry me if you were poor. I also forgot to tell you we'll have to support my mother.'

'I know, Ram. They told me.'

'And?'

'I don't care.'

I sat beside her. It was sex, the poor girl. I had been her only man and her body yearned for mine. I knew it. I knew, too, she would probably despise me later on. I told her so.

'No,' she said. 'I want to live with you. I have been bored all my life. I am just afraid of Edna and that other thing.'

'Edna is already married,' I told her.

'Is she?'

'Yes, Didi, she is.'

'And the other thing?'

'What other thing?'

'This political business. It's very dangerous, Ram. I am terribly worried about you.'

'I'll give it up,' I said.

'I am terribly in love with you,' she said.

I stood and pulled her up. 'If you love me, kiss me in front of them all.' She closed her eyes and came into my arms. We kissed and then walked hand-in-hand towards the stairs.

'Will you come home with me now?'

'No, I can't,' I said. 'I'll . . . I have to go and tell this political organization I don't belong to it any more. I shall come tomorrow and we shall spend the whole day together.' I kissed her again and put her in her car. She waved and blew me a kiss before driving away.

I walked to the Mirandi bar once more and went into the telephone booth. I dialled a number and a husky voice answered. 'Hullo, hullo?'

'Assam, you dirty dog,' I said. 'I haven't had a good game of poker for months. What? Yes, yes, I have plenty. Good; bring them and meet me at Groppi's.'

And I went to Groppi's.